Cold-Blooded Ringers

Damned Reflections, Volume 2

Julian M. Coleman

Published by Julian M. Coleman, 2021.

Also by Julian M. Coleman

Book 1
Stolen Prophet: The Prophet's Mother

Damned Reflections
The Fury of Angels
Cold-Blooded Ringers

The Demon Lover's Chronicles
Cesar
Cesar's Revenge
Rise of the Priestess

The Prophet's Mother
Malevolent Sadness: A Paranormal Suspense Thriller
Between False Shadows: A Paranormal Supernatural Thriller

Standalone

Really, Cher? A Story With a Dog in It
The Demon Lover's Chronicles (The Complete Series)

Watch for more at juliancoleman.net.

Table of Contents

To Erik, and Mina

Published in the United States by Julian M. Coleman L.L.C.

1. ESCAPE TO NYSA

*****SAMMY*****

• • • •

SAMMY WEPT. SHE WASN'T dead. She just wished she were instead of feeling his brutal sexual assault on her semi-conscious body. Death would've been better than her reality. At least the attack forced her mental escape to Nysa, which couldn't entirely blunt the violence of the rape.

Mia had warned Sammy, sort of. The diminutive overachiever had dropped a few verbal breadcrumbs before her release from Brightside Psychiatric Institute.

Mia could've said, *Hey, Sammy, there's a rapist on this floor. Watch your back.*

Sammy knew her parents had no idea they had committed their one and only child to hell. Although, she could tell from the start that Brightside wasn't all friendly faces and caring attitudes. At first, her confinement hadn't mattered because she had a plan. She would play nice for the mandatory two weeks, throw out the necessary yes ma'ams and no sirs, and then promise never to attempt suicide again. And next? Hello, freedom. Yet, she hadn't envisioned herself as rape bait.

And now, her mind screamed, *GAWD!! Please!!! Get this fucking bastard off me!!*

She wanted to beat his head in with a crowbar. Instead, she was powerless. Tears slipped down her brown face as she absorbed his less-than-tender thrusts. She wished she could resist or scream despite being strapped down and doped up.

Even now, spread-eagle and bound, she tried to awaken fully to defend herself but couldn't. The drug the unknown *he* had used to subdue her was too potent. Instead of being alert, she hovered in limbo. Luckily, her barely conscious state must've triggered her spiritual escape to paradise.

At least her arrival shielded her somewhat from the trauma.

Seated in tall grass among brightly colored flowers and casually flitting butterflies, she gazed up at the cloudless blue sky. She absorbed the soothing rays of the early morning light as a tender coating against the sexual assault suffered in the black-as-pitch hospital room. Here, she concentrated on the lavender-scented breeze heavy with moisture from the nearby river. Perhaps a stream of sunlight and the spray from the waterfall would grant her a glorious rainbow.

She slipped, momentarily, back to reality. She must've been able to cry out because the inhuman son of a bitch clamped a sweaty hand over her mouth.

Nysa. She needed to concentrate on being in Nysa.

A sigh of gratitude. It worked. Sammy returned.

The best thing about their heaven was the perpetual and glorious springtime. The idyllic utopia never had a cold day or rainfall, only a refreshing sprinkle lasting minutes and producing the most spectacular rainbows. Again with the rainbows?

Then she wondered, *Where the hell is Sara?*

Not for the first time, she wished she had never met her twin. Yet, there hadn't been an actual meeting per se because Sara had always existed as a transparent dream friend. It wasn't until their mutual near-deaths, which very nearly trapped them permanently in Nysa that the two teens met flesh-to-flesh and saw their startling resemblance.

Contrary to what her parents thought, Sara was a real person. Sammy had always known this and suspected the twins existed in different periods. She adopted the rationale that her bestie came from an alternate universe, or was that called a multiverse?

Although they were identical, Sammy lived a better existence. After all, she had fabulously well-to-do parents, worked in a vet's office, and was hopelessly crushing on a rich hunk with two last names. Nelson James.

But Sara's life, which sounded to Sammy like she lived someplace in the American midwest around the late 1800s, just plain sucked. Sara had been an outcast in her Native tribe, and the people also despised her mother, an alleged witch. Plus, her big-time medicine man dad had an outside family. Did that mean Sara's mom was the side piece?

A little over a year ago, Sammy and Sara almost died.

Sammy's near-death was – well – less traumatic. Hers was an accident. True, she had been ducking Debi, Nelson's ex, and her high-maintenance entourage when Sammy was crossing the street without looking. After that, she couldn't remember. She found out later that a professor had bounced her on the asphalt with his beat-up car.

But poor Sara? A gang of bullies almost drowned her, including the boy she thought she loved. If her older half-sister, Butterfly, hadn't interrupted their fun, Sara would've ceased to exist in both worlds. Period.

Well, that wasn't true. The creature, a Stuuwi, happened. She, or it, gave Sara the life beads which made her immortal. Sara rarely spoke about the encounter or even what the Stuuwi looked like, but Sammy could tell it scared her twin shitless. The usually fearless Sara was actually afraid of someone or something.

But it wasn't until then that Sammy realized how much their life experiences mirrored. For instance, and this was a biggie, both girls became murderers. But for different reasons.

Sammy had stopped two masked school shooters, but not before they killed a few students and her favorite teacher. The whole ordeal was a blur, but she remembered not feeling one iota of fear. She had seen an opportunity, wrestled for the high-powered rifle, and went into autopilot. BANG, BANG.

Cellphone and video footage captured her heroics. In no time, and millions of likes later, she had been anointed a social media hero. Later, guilt and her subsequent suicide attempt landed her at Brightside.

Sammy never intended to kill. It just happened. But she suspected Sara didn't mind killing because she'd always had sociopathic tendencies. Actually, Sammy knew Sara loved murdering people. It was the way Sara gleefully recounted butchering the bullies who had tried to drown her before Butterfly's rescue. Sara had hunted them one-by-one like game. And although she swore to spare him, she saved her former love interest for last.

Sammy used to cringe whenever Sara recalled cutting their throats and bathing in their blood spray. *Omigod! And yuck!*

She wondered if Sara collected trophies too. Sammy could never ask because she didn't want to know. Sara's kill-everyone mentality made Sammy regret teaching her twin how to fight using self-defense class tactics. Because of her teachings, Sara could easily throw an opponent, apply a deadly chokehold, and weaken a bastard by aiming for the soft spots.

There was a difference in their situations, though. Sammy ended up in Brightside, while Sara's life in the village had just ended.

Another tribe had attacked the Native people. But it wasn't just an attack. It was a bloody massacre. The villagers were butchered, their lodges were torched, and their livestock was either stolen or killed.

Sara hadn't gone into detail about the day she lost both parents. Sammy only remembered Sara speaking about it in an emotionless monotone. Somehow Sara escaped and found sanctuary with Butterfly, and her brutish mountain-man husband, John Colby.

Sammy shook her head as she envisioned Sara's nightmarish existence. *How fucking awful!*

There was another troubling thing the young girls had in common. Some cosmic entity in the universe, or multiverse, had given them pets. Only their companions were more than random strays. Sammy wasn't sure about Sara's experiences, but there were times when she shared an ethereal synergy with her wolf-hybrid. If Sammy were honest with herself, she would admit that Zeus behaved in a way she would imagine a witch's familiar would act.

There were times when she was emotionally dependent on her dog. Just as she suspected, Sara was attached to Midnight. Sammy smirked as she remembered how Sara told the tale of acquiring her beautiful black horse.

It was a bribe gone awry. Sara was gifted Midnight in exchange for not killing her once beloved. Although she denied her culpability in the village deaths – a big lie – she took the horse and later killed the teen anyway. Of course, she did.

Why couldn't Sammy stop thinking about her *calculating* twin?

Suddenly, she realized why with a fresh alarm. *Yes, everything happens to both of us at the same time?! Somebody's raping her, too!! Oh God, no!!*

Hot fear threaded into her bones. If Sara were here, she wouldn't hide in a place of sunshine and rainbows. Not her. In all likelihood, she squatted too close to the cliff at their sparring and target practice spot.

Sammy rose from her nurturing hideaway in the sunshine with absolute reluctance and newfound urgency. She trekked through grasslands while absorbing the lulling symphony from the crickets and colorfully plumed birds.

As she entered the forest, the terrain darkened under the canopy of thick tree limbs. Even the air was less fragrant and colder. She brushed past their favored tree, which should've borne numerous bullet holes from their many hours of practice, but was unblemished each time they returned to their Eden.

Sammy only paused long enough to run her fingers along the rough bark. This time the trunk was marred with dozens of holes—some spaced together, with others just hitting the bullseye. This find meant Sara was here.

The atmospheric coolness descended into an unaccustomed chill. A sudden and uncommon wind prickled her arms with goosebumps. Storm clouds rolled across the sky and blotted out the sun.

She wondered, *What's happening?*

As her anxieties exploded, she hugged herself and proceeded deeper into the woods. Minutes elapsed before she found Sara sitting cross-legged and too near the cliff's edge with her back facing Sammy.

Found you! Thank God! Sammy thought.

At that moment, as if reading her thoughts, Sara glanced over her shoulder, displaying her beautiful profile. Her long, dark hair shimmered in the waning sunlight. Her expression was unreadable.

"I wondered if you would come," Sara said.

"Should you sit so close to the edge?" Sammy asked as she approached with caution.

"I can't die," she answered, fingering the colorful beads around her slender throat. "In here or outside, so it doesn't matter."

Sammy experienced a singularly disgusting sensation. Beard stubble roughly sliding against her cheek. It lingered only for a moment. Reflexively, she clamped a hand over her mouth to keep from ejecting bile.

Sammy's heart pounded as she sank to her knees. He was on her, and once again, he was in her, taking what she treasured.

He's still hurting me?!!

She broke down, sobbing, as she concentrated on anchoring her soul in Nysa. She screamed, "I can still feel him fucking me...why am I not safe here!"

Suddenly, she suffered a blur of oscillating realities. In one existence, she was powerless as a faceless man stole her virginity. While in Nysa, she raced—in a slow zigzag motion—toward Sara.

Seeing her distress, Sara immediately climbed to her feet and ran to greet her. Their bodies collided, and Sara propped up Sammy in a rigid embrace.

Sammy sobbed and shook her head as she tried to disrupt the bad sensations.

"Sssh, you're with me now." Sara held her twin's head between her palms and waited for her to calm down. Although Sara didn't weep, her eyes were glossy with tears. She frowned as her brown eyes explored Sammy's.

Sara asked, in a voice throttled with emotion, "You too?"

Instantly, Sammy knew what she meant and gave a stiff nod. She had questions, but she wasn't verbal.

Sara hugged Sammy so tightly it made breathing difficult. An encompassing silence surrounded them while they remained paralyzed.

Finally, the sensations receded. After a brief eternity, Sammy softly kissed Sara's full lips. Her voice quivered as she spoke. "I can't survive this without you."

"Same." Sara released her hold and mumbled, "I've lost so much this day." She rolled her eyes skyward.

Sunlight pierced the storm clouds and shone in the forest like bright shards. The majestic sight was awe-inspiring.

Sammy had heard the biting hitch in Sara's voice. "Something worse than *this* happened?"

"Butterfly is dead." Sara stared at her hands. "Her pregnancy...the baby was breeched...I tried, but I couldn't save them...." Her voice trailed off.

"I'm so sorry," Sammy whispered. Before she could render any true comfort, her perspective shifted. Once again, the other existence began materializing, reasserting itself where woods became pale green walls and barred windows overlapped tree limbs. A transparent ceiling formed beneath the leafy branches, and the ground transmuted to puke-white tile. The suddenness was jarring and unwelcoming.

"You're fading. Stay here, with me. I can't go back yet." Sara begged.

"I wish it so," Sammy said with a determined nod. The galaxy obeyed, and Eden reformed.

A soothing rainfall drizzled from the heavens and through the fading structure. The cool droplets revitalized Sammy's spirit and dampened her misery.

"Dance with me!" Sammy stretched out her arms and twirled in the rain.

Sara's fingers entwined with hers, and they laughed and frolicked like small children.

After a time, the refreshing droplets ceased. The clouds parted, and sunlight beamed. A brilliant rainbow stretched across the sky like a gentle kiss to their heaven. The colors were spectacular, and the luminous arc appeared close enough to touch.

A flitting Monarch butterfly caused tears to well in Sara's eyes. "I love it here. I wish we could stay forever."

"Me too." Sammy thought to ask Sara who was attacking her, but the question wasn't necessary. John Colby was a useless blob of snot on the face of humanity.

A rhythmic thumping reverberated in the idyllic quiet. The distinct and thunderous sound caught Sammy's attention.

He appeared as if summoned in all his glossy blackness and galloped toward them at full speed. Sammy decided that Sara had been quite stingy in describing the magnificent black beast. Tall, massive with muscular might, narrow face, and piercing eyes. Even in his approach, he displayed immense power.

"Whoa!" Sammy was stunned when the horse came to a complete stop. He snorted and nodded at her in a way that appeared to be a greeting. He nuzzled Sara's cheek, who kissed and stroked his face with absolute tenderness.

He was so striking that Sammy smothered pangs of jealousy.

Sara said, patting his thick neck, "Midnight is the only family I have left."

Next, she made a series of tongue clicks. The horse responded by running around them in ever-widening circles before charging them at full speed. Sara ran to meet him. She collided against his body and vaulted upward in a graceful jump before plopping onto the saddle. It was physical poetry.

Once she grabbed hold of the reins, the steed reared, his forelegs clawing the air, and then he gracefully shifted downward and effortlessly wove through the copse of trees. With each gallop, the pair faded until they both disappeared.

"Did she just leave me here? Goddamit, Sara!" Sammy fumed.

Her anger melted when Zeus materialized next to the bullet-riddled tree. His sudden appearance caused her to gasp. Having him alongside her in paradise caused her heart to thump with joy. She knelt until they were face-to-face. She couldn't help it. She cried. Again. She was so tired of crying.

"Did I pull you into this world? Or am I dreaming?" She hugged him, and he licked her face. "Nope, I'm not dreaming!"

His brown eyes locked with hers. Suddenly, they were communicating, and he had something to reveal.

She glimpsed images that flickered like movies from an old reel as she witnessed the world through the eyes of her canine. And Zeus presented a nighttime and outside view of Brightside.

"When is this?" she asked. "Tonight?"

She felt a *yes* answer.

A subsequent scene showed him *(them)* hiding in bushes. He waited. A figure emerged from the building. Zeus sniffed the air.

Her perspective switched. Now she observed with an omnipotent detachment as the dog tracked a man, with predatory stealth, to the employee parking lot.

"Is that him, boy?"

Again, she felt a *yes* answer.

Amid the surrounding darkness, the glowing white globe on a green lamppost revealed the face of the man, her assailant, as he beeped the unlocking mechanism to his Nissan.

Sammy gasped. Can't be? Sweet, friendly Roger, who had given her the nickel tour when she'd first arrived at the psychiatric facility?

She saw how Roger looked around nervously before sliding into the driver's seat.

Zeus hesitated.

Instinctively, she knew he awaited a command.

But she wasn't like Sara. She didn't think she could kill or be involved in killing without remorse. Although at that moment, she was willing to give it a gung-ho try.

But what of her cherished familiar?

There were strategically placed cameras inside the hospital. Sammy assumed there were others outside as well. She couldn't take the chance of putting Zeus in danger. Tracking him down was a remote possibility but still a possibility. Once found, he faced euthanization. She couldn't risk it.

"Go home," she said in a whisper. "We will deal with him later."

2. REPRISAL

*****SARA*****

• • • •

THE BEADS AROUND HER neck first tingled, then throbbed with the persistent rhythm of a heartbeat.

Sara awakened. She was stiff with cold; her teeth chattered, and she struggled to flex her muscles or bend her joints. Frigidity drilled through her bones and right into her marrow.

Her face was partially buried in snow. She needed to get up before she died again.

But her limbs were leaden and initially uncooperative, despite her will. After a few half-hearted tries, she slowly moved her hands under her torso. Then, with a weak push, she lifted her face out of the iciness.

From afar, she heard Midnight neighing persistently. His mighty hooves stomped as if trying to force her awake.

Again, she tried to rise but still couldn't muster the strength. She wanted to sleep. Finally, she surveyed the area and saw a bloody trail leading from the cabin to her where she lay. There was so much of it, and she knew she should've died.

Had she?

Anger gave her strength. She pushed herself upright. Pain ripped through her head. Her throat hurt. She couldn't dare swallow.

She remembered how John Colby startled her with a savage blow to her forehead, and while she was barely conscious, the bastard had raped her steps from his dead wife and child.

She realized the blood didn't just belong to her when she saw two crimson snow-covered lumps. Alone, in the crisp night, she wept. They'd all been tossed like trash.

She regained her composure, and Midnight, possibly sensing her movements, settled down in the stable.

When she felt strong enough, she climbed to her feet, wobbling until she steadied. She took a few hesitant steps while maintaining her balance and remaining upright. Then she snuck to the cabin and peered inside.

A fire was dying in the hearth but emitted enough light to show a room in disarray. John Colby had fallen asleep with his head resting on the table and a hand wrapped around a bottle.

As quiet as a ghost, she crept to the door and gave a gentle push. Once it opened, she slipped inside the room.

The only sound was the drunkard's bleating snores.

Sara was unarmed. She hated being vulnerable without a weapon. She couldn't risk searching for her knife. Instead, her attention focused on the bed. The sheets, as well as the surrounding dirt floor, were covered in blood and afterbirth.

Sara froze as she relived the final moments of her sister's life. On the floor near the bed lay her blood-covered knife.

Guilt knotted her guts. Her desire for revenge evaporated as she yielded to the totality of her loss. Her mom was dead, and her dad, and now her sister. She screamed silently.

Midnight neighed again. The sound unlocked her stupor just as she realized the snoring had stopped.

Instinctively she lunged for the knife and landed in a drying pool of Butterfly's blood.

John Colby aimed his gun. Sara threw her knife. Before he could squeeze off a shot, the blade split his skin and sliced into his torso. Although she missed his heart, he went down, sputtering blood.

Sara hadn't wanted him to die. Not yet. He moaned and writhed on the floor. His fingers clutched the gun in a weak grip. It wavered as he tried to aim it at her.

First, she kicked the gun out of his hand. Then she sauntered over to the table and helped herself to a swig of his liquor. The taste was bitter, and the liquid burned her throat until she coughed, but it also warmed her insides better than any blazing hearth fire.

She rolled her eyes back, rapidly batting them. In this way, she sent a visual image to her horse, who subsequently quieted.

"You must be hungry," she said out loud.

"I need a doctor!" John moaned.

Sara smirked. "I'm not talking to you." She took another swig.

Then she settled the bottle on the table and climbed atop his prone body with her knees pinning his arms to the floor.

"Ow!"

Blood gushed from his wound. His eyes rolled in his head. Sara slapped his face to get his attention. His expression was full of venom.

"Let's begin," Sara said. She yanked out the blade and plunged it into his arm. She absorbed his screams like sweet music.

• • • •

THE WINTER WAS HARSH in the gulch. The mountains insulated the cabin, but the constant snowstorms covered the area in a pristine white blanket.

Butterfly had prepared provisions for two, so there were enough food and wood for the long and terrible months. Sara admired her sister's foresight and understood why John Colby had kept her as his wife despite never showing her a morsel of love.

Sara's only issue was ensuring that Midnight and his companion, Bailey, were warm and well-fed.

During her extended stay with Butterfly and John, the pair had never entertained a single visitor, so she was confident she could remain undisturbed until spring.

After torturing and killing John, she honored Butterfly and her unnamed son. She built a small pyre, bound mother and son together in clean cloths, and set it afire.

Her mother would've said a prayer to Obatala. Her father would've danced, thus alerting the Great Spirit of their arrival. Sara was stoic in her grief as the flames raged under gray skies. With her revenge appeased, she couldn't dredge up any emotion. She watched as meat and bone turned to ash. It took days for the fragments to disintegrate completely. She shoveled their remains into a pot, walked downstream, and sprinkled mother and babe into the waters.

The day after she murdered John Colby, she dragged his body to the trash heap where he'd thought he had discarded her and the others. She left him to rot while she tended to Butterfly and her son's funeral.

When she'd returned, she saw gouges and teeth marks where the scavengers had eaten. She stared into his vacant eye sockets and sneered.

The missing eyes? That was her work. She'd scooped them out after she had severed his man parts.

Now she stood over his naked, partially devoured body and sighed. She regarded the corpse with a bit of curiosity. The day was cold yet beautiful. Perhaps the climate had frozen him enough to make his dismemberment easy? She wished she could leave him to the animals, but she couldn't allow his carcass to lure wolves or bears.

She thought of what Sammy would say.

Any excuse, Sara, any damn excuse. You know you want to cut him to pieces.

Still, she savored the memory of his death. His cries of eternal pain and endless suffering lingered in her mind like a favored song. Then, with a hardened heart and a humorless smile, she swung the ax and severed his neck.

3. LITTLE RUTHIE

SARA

• • • •

SHE HAD NEVER BEEN alone before and was growing accustomed to never hearing another human voice. The winter was quiet. To her, the world was dead.

As the months elapsed and her abdomen swelled, Sara wanted to die too. On the darkest winter day, her energy and will to live withered once she realized she was pregnant.

She wanted the baby growing in her womb to die. She stopped eating. She slept most days into the night and nibbled when the urge to eat was overpowering. She sought Sammy when visiting Nysa. But as pleasant and as peaceful heaven seemed, it was another hell without her twin.

Maybe, she wondered, *maybe Sammy is going through the same thing.*

The thought was too disturbing, and Sara stopped visiting their sanctuary.

Midnight, as if sharing her sorrow, stopped eating despite her pleas. Gradually, his coat lost its magnificent luster, and his bones protruded. Whenever she ate just a bit, so did Midnight.

Damn horse.

Worse than her horse's emotional blackmail were the nightmares. In them, she saw the something being who resembled her mother, a sprite with soot covering her features, flaming eye sockets, and a fiery plume for hair. The Stuuwi. Like a nocturnal she-demon, she watched through the cabin windows with a ferocity only matched by the flames dancing around her skull. In every dream, she always scratched the thin glass with bloody fingernails.

Sara, the killer, the brave warrior, shrank under her blankets and wept in her dreams. Each time, she said the same prayer.

You're not my mother. You're Stuuwi, the Trickster.

No, a voice she didn't recognize hissed in her mind. *You're the trickster. I know what you don't know. Why are you afraid of me? Is it because you think I'm ugly? Or is it because you sense the truth?*

Sara was adamant in her convictions. *You're the trickster! There is no other truth!*

She would awaken from those horrific dreams biting down on bloodcurdling screams. But were they dreams? The lingering scent of smoldering flesh was unmistakable. The Stuuwi's presence was tangible, and Sara's unwavering glare moved from corner to corner with the speed of a solitary blink. By the time the dawn's light filled the cabin, Sara was paralyzed with fear.

"Leave me alone!" Each time she pleaded, the only response was silence. Only once did she think she heard a reply.

I'm here to help you, Witch.

Sara erupted with humorless laughter. She remembered when others called her mother a witch. Then again, maybe some part of Sara believed the Stuuwi. If she acted as if those words were truth, the burnt woman might leave her alone.

After all, what choice did she have?

• • • •

SHE WAS GOING TO DIE alone, in a cursed cabin, on the same bed Butterfly had birthed her dead son, with Sara's help. The gods were paying her back. It was the only explanation for her predicament.

By the time spring finally arrived, her food stores were nearly bare. The stream provided fresh fish. She found seeds and replanted Butterfly's garden. The work was tedious, more so because of her girth, but sweet vegetables were worth the effort. Even Midnight liked the carrots, although he was reluctant to share them with Bailey.

Still, fish and a few vegetables weren't enough. Thoughts of going into town and stocking up on supplies were a dangerous plan, but she had few alternatives. She needed necessities like flour and salt.

One summer morning, a viperous pain uncoiled inside her body. She screamed, cried, begged, and cajoled in her delirium. Her only hope was a quick death. She curled on the bed and writhed as sweat soaked her skin and blankets. Would she die like Butterfly? Fluid seeped from the opening between her thighs. She parted her legs and felt the babe's scalp. She laughed and cried before passing out from the blood loss.

She was delusional. In her madness, it was already nightfall. She expected the demonic Stuuwi to taunt her with stupid riddles. The stench of singed flesh evaporated into her mother's familiar and comforting scent.

Your power called me. I am here.

Someone lifted her head and forced cool water down her throat. Her cracked lips stung, but the liquid was so sweet she didn't mind. A cold cloth was pressed on her forehead.

Wracked by another pain, she released an endless bellow. She knew she was hallucinating when she felt the whisper of a kiss on her cheek.

Although she began mumbling incoherently, she had one thought. She uttered, "I don't want to live. I want to die."

You can't. A raspy voice injected, *You must live. I will always help you when I can. I do this for the future. I know what you don't know.*

"Don't touch me," she gasped, shuddering in fear, before passing out again.

• • • •

SARA AWAKENED.

She looked around, stunned.

Magic?

The cabin had been swept clean and neatly rearranged. A bundle twitched at her side. She delicately pulled aside the newborn's swaddling cloth and counted fingers and toes. The babe, a girl, was rewrapped and tucked under her arm, where she latched onto Sara's nipple and suckled.

Around the child's neck was a beaded necklace, a smaller version of hers. Sara stared at it in wonder. Then, with an index finger, she tugged at the leather rope holding the beads together. The necklace elongated, and white, smoky balls formed on the extended places. Light swirled within the new spheres until they solidified into tiny multicolored orbs.

Sara gasped. Not magic, but witchcraft. All of it. The care shown to her and the child, the cleanliness of the cabin, and even the aromatic food cooking in the pot hanging over the hearth had to be the handiwork of a mother caring for her incapacitated child.

But the Stuuwi? How could that be?

She released the necklace and watched as the orbs disappeared and the strand shrank around the child's neck.

Delicately, she placed the newborn on the bed and searched for the knife. She found it on the table among the cutlery. She examined the gleaming blade. Once covered with nicks and blunted at the tip from excessive use, it now looked new.

She hurried back to the babe, grabbed a section of the necklace, which again elongated in her grip, and sawed. And sawed. And sawed.

She tested the blade on her nightshirt. It sliced the fabric with ease. She returned to her earlier task and sawed the leather strand again, this time with vigor. She examined the space between the beads. As far as she could tell, the necklace was impervious to her efforts.

Exhausted, Sara tucked the sleeping child under the thin sheet and helped herself to the food. And as she devoured the stew, she communicated with Midnight.

The horse showed her a pictorial view of a clean environment. She sensed his full belly and the cool temperatures in the stable, a reprieve from the scorching hot day.

Sara upended the bowl and slurped the remains. Her attention drifted back to the babe. She had to be rid of it. There was no way she could care for a child.

Remembering the Stuuwi filled her with dread. She always taunted Sara with the same words. *I know what you don't know.*

4. RETRIBUTION

ZEUS

• • • •

IT WAS LATE.

Although bowls of fresh water and tasty kibbles were available for his nourishment, Zeus remained uncomfortable and unhappy. He missed the girl and only left her bedroom after the older humans departed. Tonight, he sniffed acute sourness from the male human as he moved about the house.

The large door slammed shut, followed by the faint sound of metallic jangles.

Zeus lifted the blinds with his nose and peered through the girl's bedroom window. The male human whistled as he climbed inside his rolling machine.

The older female human had been gone for some time. Zeus liked her, but only sadness sweated from her meat.

Zeus climbed onto the girl's bed and reveled in her residual scent. Usually, he languished with his head on her pillows. But this time, he sensed he had to leave home, too.

He left the room, descended the stairs, and crept out of the house through the pet door. Once outside, he leaped onto a box containing gardening supplies and used it as a springboard to bound over the fence.

He was fierce. His hunt was primal. As he often did at night, he trotted, daring traffic while his demeanor scared the few pedestrians who wandered in his path. Tonight he was determined. He knew something was wrong, and he also knew he had to hurry.

His trek was arduous. The winding miles caused his paws to ache. This time he'd gotten further along before the throbbing bore into his pads and shimmied up his legs. He had learned from past near-accidents how to dodge the rolling machines before their white eyes could blind him.

Instead of the multiple-row place where the rolling things traveled in packs, he took shortcuts through wooded spaces and used a route where few machines honked. He knew he was close to the girl when he reached a familiar yet isolated stretch of land.

The structure of many doors and many windows loomed above the shadows. Zeus didn't like the sharp smell of the place. There were many unpleasant odors, but the combination of salt, alkaline, and sulfur caused him tremendous sadness. The girl was inside, and he knew she wasn't happy either.

But tonight, she was scared, too. He stared helplessly through the bars and wished he could get closer, but the gates and high walls blocked his access.

Zeus plodded the perimeter with restless agony. Someone had filled the deep hole he'd dug the previous evening. He drove his nose in the dirt, felt it was still soft, and began burrowing again.

A sudden flash of an image caused him to stop. Zeus raised his head, pricked his ears, and shook the dirt off his nose. More liquid bits lapped over his vision. Primarily, he saw darkness. Then he saw a face and hands. His ears rotated upward in high alert as he tasted her terror. He realized someone was forcing her to mate.

He sensed the girl's ignorance at sending the pictures.

Suddenly, her screams filled his mind. He growled.

Zeus! Then she sensed him.

He frantically paced as he barked and then howled, and Sammy sensed that he wanted to kill.

No!

Through pictures, she commanded otherwise. *Cameras,* she thought. *I can't lose you.* Then she shut him out.

Zeus paced again, more desperately, because he knew she was suffering. He had to get inside and save her.

He saw a figure approach. Initially, he drew back his ears and snarled. Then he relaxed when he recognized the familiar scent. He liked the bulky man whose heartbeat was irregular and who sweated looming sickness.

"Sssh, hey! Pipe down! Weren't you here last night?"

The human reached through the bars and rubbed the sweet place between his ears. Zeus responded by wagging his tail. He wanted in, badly.

The human held a bag that leaked meaty juices. He sighed as he looked over at Zeus' tunneling.

"Digging again, too? Which one of these rich nutcases belongs to you?" He laughed, then he said, "The administrator's scared of you because you're a big guy, but we both know you're a pussy."

He reached through the bars, flipped to the backside of Zeus' identification tag, and shined a light on the address. Sighing heavily, he said, "You came all this way? If you stay here, I can take you home when I get off my shift. Deal?" He looked Zeus squarely in the eye. "But you can't keep coming back. Ain't safe for you." He reached out his hand.

Zeus lifted his paw, and they shook on it.

"Good boy." He said, "We don't want anyone to hurt you." Then he opened his bag.

Zeus licked his chops and, with utmost restraint, waited for the bulky human to pass a portion of his sandwich between the bars.

He was gentle as he picked the offering out of the human's hand, placed it on the ground, and devoured it with relish.

"Glad you liked it. I can barely stomach my wife's meatloaf." The human patted his head again. "Well, I guess you're my entertainment for the evening. I gotta make my rounds. Be good."

Zeus watched him disappear inside the building. His thoughts returned to her, and he wanted in. Now he sensed she was asleep, but her disturbing thoughts told him she thought she wasn't safe.

Suddenly, her scent was outside the building. Perplexed, Zeus wondered how she could be outside when she was inside, too. He tracked the new smell. A male stood at a boxy machine, opened the door, and climbed inside.

Zeus realized the new aroma wasn't pure. He smelled male mating fluid and blood. *Her* blood. The blood scent enraged him.

The rolling box sped toward the gate. The male's arm waved over a metal pole, and then the gate opened wide.

The machine zoomed past.

Zeus ran, but not toward the building where the girl stayed. Instead, he followed the grumbling machine.

The night was chilly. The bloody mating smells, camouflaged by gasoline and rubber, didn't entirely dissipate. The male kept his window down, and Zeus followed the aroma thread despite almost losing him a few times. He was lucky, too, because the rolling box never joined the pack places where the rolling things and their confusing olfactory smorgasbords zipped at incredible speeds.

Zeus tired early in the chase. His paws bled after running over glass shards. After a time, he became tired and angry. He had no choice but to draw down in the dirt and rest. Just as he was giving up, he caught a fresh waft of the particular aroma.

He ran toward a building surrounded by bright lights where many humans entered or exited, toting food bags.

The male emerged from the meat place wearing her smell along with the odor of oily meat. Zeus whined from stifled rage. He wanted to pounce, to rip and tear, but he knew he had to be cautious.

The male climbed inside his machine and rolled away.

Although he was exhausted, Zeus was on the trail. The male didn't travel far. The boxy machine rolled to a stop at a small, isolated house. Zeus scouted the area and surmised access to the male looked easier.

The door groaned open.

A snarl rumbled up Zeus's throat. He sank low on his haunches and crept closer.

The male climbed out of the machine. His happy whistling pierced Zeus' psyche. Then, with a narrowed stare, he watched the male walk toward the home.

Growling low in his throat, Zeus pounced.

Food and something rattling flew out of the man's hands when Zeus stood on his hind legs and clawed gashes into the enemy's chest. Fresh blood heightened his fury. He sank his teeth into supple flesh and ripped out chunks of muscle.

A solitary scream echoed in the night.

Zeus clamped his teeth in the male's throat and tore out the sound. Blood erupted from his mouth. As the male gurgled, Zeus dug his sharp claws into his chest and tore away more meat.

The male gasped once. His eyes stared at the sky, and then his heart stopped beating.

Still exhausted, Zeus lifted his leg and pissed on him. Then he trotted back to the street to get his bearings.

He wandered the remainder of the night, confused, wounded, and tired. When sunrise washed the landscape in light, he saw how much blood covered his coat. He sat next to a road and licked an aching paw.

Tires squealed, and a passing rolling machine stopped. A young male approached him with caution. Zeus saw an opportunity. He limped, favoring one of his wounded paws, and whined.

"What happened? Are you okay?" The male held up his hands as he continued to advance.

Zeus whined louder and licked the male's hand.

"Oh, look at you." His voice filled with sympathy. "Did you get hit? Did you get in a fight?"

He examined the tag on the collar. "Hmm, I guess I can take you home. It's not too far out the way."

The stranger helped Zeus onto the back seat of his rolling box. Inside smelled of baby puke and poo. These were comfortable scents, and instantly, he fell asleep.

The boxy machine rolled to a stop. Zeus lifted an eyelid when the young human climbed out and slammed the door close with a hard bang.

Zeus, suddenly alert, raised his head and peered out the window.

He was home.

The male rang the doorbell. Zeus knew no one would be home.

The human returned, exasperated. He plopped inside the machine and pressed a button. "Siri, where's the nearest veterinary hospital?"

A voice pitched a little too harshly for his hearing and said, "Here is the nearest veterinary hospital, 132 Oakdale Drive."

"Shit, I'm going to be late."

The machine moved, but soon after, they stopped. Here, the scents were pleasantly familiar, and Zeus wagged his tail.

Again, the strange male left, but this time he returned with someone Zeus knew.

Marsha peered inside the car. The girl liked Marsha, which meant that he liked her too. His tail thumped harder on the upholstery.

"You're right. He's one of ours. Can you help me get him inside? I'm an old woman, and my back ain't what it used to be."

The male protested. "Don't you have assistants? I have to be in a meeting in twenty minutes?"

"You're a good Samaritan, ain't cha? Our assistant ain't here yet."

The male sweated and strained as he hoisted Zeus onto the table.

"Damn, he's got blood all over my clothes!"

Zeus was carried inside and placed on a table.

"Thank you," Marsha said. She gave the man some wipes and hustled the cursing male out the door.

Marsha smirked, "Hey, Zeus, whatcha get mixed up in? Was it a squirrel or an evil fence?"

She pressed a button on a small box on a table. Then, in a flash, the big picture box lit up with faces and voices flooding the room.

"Doc will be here in a little bit." She gingerly ran her fingers down his fur. The tips came away slick with blood.

Zeus sat up and stared into her eyes.

"You ain't injured," Marsha said. "Where did you get all this blood? You been fighting another dog? Let me get you some water."

When she was gone, a voice from the picture box said, "...investigators believe he was attacked outside his home...."

5 THE SLEEPER

SAMMY

• • • •

SHE HEARD VOICES. HISSING, angry words intruded into the protective cloud of sleep. Shifting in bed, she tried to block out the burgeoning loudness of the conversation.

She wanted to drift once again into oblivion, but her father's insistent baritone penetrated the murkiness. His berating sarcasm was full of vicious contempt, and his vocal explosions were punctuated with an occasional ironic laugh.

A woman, whose voice was barely familiar, spoke in a subservient way as she pleaded for understanding since the alleged offender was dead.

Offender? Dead?

Sammy twitched at interposing memories. Horrible memories. If she were lucky, she would emerge in Nysa surrounded by flowers, bathing in sunlight and listening to a vibrant waterfall.

Sammy caught a whiff of her mother's favorite cologne and turned toward the scent.

"Barry, keep your voice down!" Joyce admonished.

Her heart thumped, hopefully.

Mom?

She couldn't help it; she was awakening to a reality too harsh to contemplate.

"Please, let's continue this conversation in my office."

Now more aware, she recognized the voice of the hospital administrator, Dr. Marshall.

"Continue what? That monster raped my baby girl on your watch. You owe us more than free care! You promised to fix her!" Barry bellowed.

Joyce wept loudly.

"I didn't say we could fix her," Dr. Marshall countered. "She's not a broken toy."

Sammy wanted to disappear as memories asserted over the comfortable darkness. Could she forget how Mai had warned her days before her discharge?

She remembered the brutal assault. Roger. Of all people, the sweet, smiling, friendly Roger had filled her with an armful of drugs and taken her virginity.

Thank God he's dead, she thought.

Her stay at Brightside Psychiatric Hospital extended beyond the court-appointed ten days.

The rape had left her despondent, and Sammy was nonverbal, even after her mom had arrived.

Joyce had insisted on a physical examination, which revealed the brutality of her rape.

She wanted to forget, even now, as her dad fervently argued with the blathering administrator. If only Sammy could speak her pain, she knew she could alleviate some of the hurt. But a part of her also knew the horror weighed too much to express in simple words.

"What are you giving her? She's a zombie. When are you going to make her better?" Barry bellowed.

"Please," Dr. Marshall said. "Let's talk in my office. I believe she's coming around."

The arguments dwindled as the trio moved beyond earshot.

At least Roger was gone. Dead. Had someone mentioned a savage attack? No one brought up Zeus' name. At least her beloved found a way to end her suffering without getting caught.

FOR MONTHS SHE BARELY slept. Food had no taste. Sammy withered.

The doctors fed her more drugs to address the dismal changes in her behavior. By now, she drifted in and out of a melancholy stupor. The staff usually rolled her in a wheelchair to the Common Room, where she deteriorated by the windows. They treated her like a houseplant.

One day a nurse noticed her protruding abdomen while giving her a sponge bath. Soon after, the doctors ran tests. She was pregnant.

Sammy had been too grief-stricken to notice any bodily changes. Naturally, the news shattered her spirit. She became a lost soul chemically numbed with narcotics to the sad circumstances of her existence.

The only times she experienced a sliver of happiness was when her beautiful wolf-hybrid visited. Somehow, he had found a way onto the grounds. On those days when the hospital staff didn't chase him away, he would sit opposite her with only the plexiglass separating them. He had kind eyes. Her thin fingers ached to touch his magnificent coat.

She would work her cracked lips to talk to him, but the words lodged in her throat. She could only whimper and slobber.

What was the dog's name again? *Are you mine?*

She seemed to remember his visit to the magical place. But with time, that memory grew fuzzier and less real. Still, she wished she could remember what she called the heavenly sanctuary. Maybe if she recollected the name, she could go back.

The wolfish dog always came back. There was something supernatural about him too. Sometimes Sammy thought she saw the outside world through his eyes. His images told her how he lived with her mom and dad. How they rarely spoke to each other. He seemed to prefer to stay at the vet's office when he wasn't trying to visit with her—what was this place again?

In her mind's eye, she saw him with a heavyset woman. Marsha. Her name was Marsha. She took him in and loved him as her own.

You're safe. Is your name Zeus?

Staying awake meant staying aware, and eventually, while he watched, she would fall asleep in the pool of sunshine streaming through the window. When she woke up alone in her room, she would *always* feel the tremendous loss of him.

Finally, with a heavy heart, she begged *Zeus. Please don't come back. I can't bear it.*

The hybrid did her bidding and stopped appearing. She missed him terribly as her life continued to lose its luster.

Like Zeus, Nelson James, the smoldering heartthrob with the soft gray eyes, visited. His screaming outrage insinuated the depth of her deterioration.

"I need to get you out of this damn hospital!" he shouted. "I knew something was wrong when they wouldn't let me see you! Jesus Christ! I will talk to my father and get you out of here!"

Sammy remembered being lucid during their conversation. His tenderness was more than she could bear, and she sobbed in earnest. Yes, his family was wealthy, but her father had the law on his side.

"I'm glad that bastard is dead, or I would've killed him," he said through clenched teeth.

Speaking remained challenging for Sammy, but she managed to say, "That's the only good thing." She stroked her protruding abdomen.

Nelson asked, "What are you going to do? Are you keeping it?"

How many times had she asked herself the same question? She stared into his eyes and escaped answering by disappearing inside her soul.

"Sammy? Can you hear me?"

Nelson's voice sounded farther and farther away. Later, when she was alone in her room, she wondered if she'd imagined his visit. Or had it been a dream?

Her only links to the outside world were her nauseatingly apologetic parents, especially after DNA testing proved the rapist was the father of her baby. Afterward, she heard conversations between her parents about a lawsuit.

Again, she made the news. At least, that's what she overheard from a conversation between a few staff members. Because of her case, others had stepped up to sue the hospital.

Mai.

One evening, late in her pregnancy, Sammy was overwhelmed by the inner tsunami of debilitating emotions. Forever, it seemed, she screamed, wept, and raged. She had caused such a fuss the nurse had her strapped to her bed and sedated.

Since she'd been weaned off drugs, her lucidity made her situation intolerable. She remembered Nysa. She knew the magical place offered an escape from her dreary life. Maybe it was the drugs. Perhaps she wasn't doing something right. But no matter how she tried, she couldn't materialize into paradise.

She wondered about Sara. Had her twin been impregnated by her rapist, too?

On those nights when the baby kicked her awake, she wondered if Sara was real. Had she created a badass version of herself to cope in a complicated world?

Her doctor *thought* he had nailed it by saying, "Who doesn't have dreams of an idyllic world to hide in when life turns harsh?"

She had to admit Sara was like a superhero who didn't take shit and killed anyone who got in her way. God, she wished she was a fighter like her best friend.

Sammy had hoped the brouhaha surrounding her pregnancy would be her route home. Instead, the orderlies transferred her to a larger room equipped with a private television. Her new accommodations only deepened her depression, and she further withdrew by sleeping more.

Her parents visited, usually accompanied by Dr. Marshall, but their stay usually ended with her dad complaining about her condition. Of course, that was his modus operandi. He blustered and bullied whenever he felt insecure or helpless.

Why couldn't she go home?

During one of their impromptu drop-ins, and while her dad spent a half-hour shouting at Dr. Marshall to fix his daughter, Sammy felt a sharp abdominal stab.

"Why is she still a damn zombie!" Barry yelled.

"I agree she's mentally deteriorating, but there's nothing we can do until after she has the baby."

She said, sobbing, "I'm right here. I can hear everything you're saying! You act like I'm not in the same room!" Then she grunted and doubled over as pain ripped her midsection.

"Is it time?" Joyce shouted, startled.

A flurry of activity cycled around her as the ache seized her like an impenetrable vise. Fluid dribbled from her vagina.

Her mother held her hand as she was placed on a gurney and wheeled inside an ambulance. Someone, a man with a cherry face and a redder crop of hair, asked about her contractions.

In a blur, she was rushed inside a hospital and attached to machines. Then some asshole stabbed her in the back with a needle. Mercifully, the pain subsided.

A wide mirror hung overhead, and with her mother by her side, she witnessed the miraculous birth of her son. He was beautiful.

"Hello, Trevor," she said with an exhausted smile.

6. THE BLACKSMITH

****SARA*****

• • • •

SARA HEARD THE DISTANT galloping horses. Soon after, she smelled their stench, presumably dried dung wafting from their dirty garbs. And then she heard their boisterous chatter.

It was late summer, and she had been tending the little garden adjacent to the cabin when she was momentarily paralyzed by their noisy entrance.

No-Name was less than two months old, and Sara had left her babe babbling in a makeshift crib.

Before being spotted, she dropped the hoe and climbed inside through a side window. Then she bolted the door, snatched her fidgety offspring from the crib, and pressed her back against the wall.

She tasted fear for the first time in months, but not for herself. She feared for the child she refused to bless with a name. She had gotten too comfortable in her isolation.

"Hey! John! Where you at, Boy? Poking the squaw?"

The raps on the door were insistent. Sara made herself as small as possible when she saw a shadow passing the window.

"Mike, I don't see nuthin'!"

Another voice said, "Got two horses in the back. Cain't be too far."

More knocks, harder, and more persistent.

Sara surmised there were three, perhaps four men. In another life, she could've taken them, but now?

"He ain't here! Don't see his squaw either? House looked too clean for a injun raid. Something ain't right, though."

Nearby, someone hawked and spat. "John ain't just up and quit drinking. His traps look beat up. Ain't been used in a coon's age. 'Sides, the bastard owes me money. Better git the sheriff up here."

The men made noisy jokes about Ol' John Colby's lust for drinking, whoring, and gambling, but not in that sequence, yuk, yuk, yuk. Their crude recollections faded as they rode in the direction of town.

Sara's heart thumped. Her peaceful life of solitude was over. Her babe looked up with unfocused eyes. A pure emotion tugged at her heart. Love.

Her attention drifted to the necklace around the infant's throat. Had she made the necklace and forgotten about it because of the fever? What about the one she'd found threaded through Midnight's mane? Where had that come from, or had she done that too?

Or did she believe in spirits?

She inspected the cabin. Tears moistened her eyes. It was over. Mentally, she said goodbye.

Prepare yourself, she thought to Midnight, who whinnied in response.

The solemn truth was she had no place to go. Then she remembered the shiny-faced black man who had spoken kindly to her when John Colby had tried to sell her off. A kind soul in a rundown town. Perhaps he could help her again.

She tossed some of their belongings in a sack, along with water, food, and items for No-Name. While holding her bundle close to her heart with one hand, she led the horses out of their stalls and guided them to a small hill. She swaddled the baby in a leather and fur bag lashed securely to Midnight's saddle.

She returned to the cabin for a final look-see and saw nothing else she needed from the place.

Dousing lamp oil on the meager furnishings, she struck a match and lit up her home. She tossed the lamp into the growing pyre and watched, mesmerized, as the flames ate the wooden structure like a greedy entity.

Midnight whinnied, drawing her from the almost hypnotic lure of the fire. She returned to the waiting horses, tested the straps' security, and kissed the top of her daughter's curly head. Thus, she began her arduous trek to the town.

She walked. It was a calculated risk, but she thought she would receive less scrutiny than if she rode a horse.

Once the path meandered out of the gulch, the terrain turned flat with little brush to provide cover. Midnight, carrying No-Name, led their way. She anticipated the return of the smelly riders. She kept one hand on Bailey's reins, and the other lingered near the six-shooter. She only stopped to care for the baby's needs but remained on continuous alert. She was hopeful the magic in the beads would protect them. Only poor Bailey was unencumbered by any form of enchantment.

It was late when they reached the edge of town. Sara heard carousing up the road. Singing and revelry emanated from the brightly lit saloon. A man, weaving on bent legs, strode through the swinging doors and onto the wooden sidewalk and puked.

The other timber-framed structures on the broad street were dark except for the small light within the blacksmith's shop.

She approached the building cautiously, hoping for more of the giant man's kindness. Overwhelmed by fatigue, she rapped on the door. No-Name fretted with fussy cries. She heard heavy, lumbering footsteps advancing to the door.

She pulled the child out of her cradle and pressed a hand at its bottom. Wet and clumpy.

The door opened, and she faced the barrel of a rifle. The big man's eyes were wide with fright.

"You. I remember you. You is Mistah John Colby's gal."

She said, "I remember you too, Clyde."

He relaxed his hold on the gun and aimed the rifle at the floor. Then he peered around outside and looked back at her before asking, "You in trouble?"

"Yes."

Sara understood fear. Nevertheless, she was astounded by how anyone as tall and powerfully built as he could ever be afraid of anyone.

Again, he scanned the night. Satisfied, he stood aside and allowed them to come inside his workshop. He steered her past a brick forge covered with soot, a large set of bellows atop an anvil, and an array of tools hung on a far wall with bent nails.

They went through another doorway to a living area. The rooms were smaller and sparsely furnished. The main room only had a table, a couple of chairs, and a bed.

"You hungry?" he asked in a deep voice that was as calming as a lake.

"Yes," she said and placed the babe on the bed. "And may I have some water to wash my child?" she asked.

He filled a jug from a pump mounted on the counter. He poured some water into a basin and the rest into a cup. Sara took the cup and drained it in three noisy gulps. Then backhanded her mouth and proceeded to her task.

He loomed over them both.

She took a bit of cloth from the sack around her waist, dipped it into the basin, and washed the babe.

Clyde said, "You still beautiful. I remember when that louse, Mistah Colby, came here tryin' to sell you. Miss Nadine would've worked you to death in her whorehouse. She died last year. Folk say she be poisoned. I don't get in white folks' business, tho. They got a new madam now, Miss Violet. She be real nice."

Sara sat in the chair, opened her shirt to reveal a brown nipple, and promptly nursed her child. Clyde licked his lips.

She needed an ally in the hostile environment. Sex was a small price to pay.

"You say you is hungry? I fix you up something."

Her stomach grumbled at the mention of food.

"Got some leftover mush. I ain't much of a cook. I git my food from Miss Nellie's. She got a rooming house in Darkie Town. It's down the way yonder. She a good Christian woman. I think she kinda sweet on me too."

He tee-hee'd before disappearing and returning with a bowl of mush and a spoon. He placed the items on the table. Still toting her babe, she slid onto the chair, smiled her gratitude, and shoveled food into her mouth.

"You go on and finish eatin'. I'll take care of your horses." He said and lumbered out of the room.

Under different circumstances, she would've protested anyone touching Midnight. But for some reason, she trusted him.

Sara finished the offering without tasting the food, which she considered a good thing because it looked like a foul concoction of limp vegetables and near-rancid deer meat.

No-Name slept with her little lips clamped on Sara's nipple. Sara tenderly separated them, checked her to see if another change was needed, and then placed her gingerly atop the small bed.

She heard a presence. Within seconds, her hand automatically drew her six-shooter, and she aimed at Clyde's heart.

"Damn!" He held his hands up in defense. "It's jist me. You sho is fast with that thing."

She holstered the gun, a smile lifting a corner of her lips.

"I done seen the other horse is Bailey. I shoed him many times, so I know him." He asked sternly, "What 'cha doing with Bailey? No man go give up his horse. Horse thieves hang in these parts."

"John Colby is dead," she said without emotion. And she added, "I need money, and I want to sell Bailey."

Clyde dropped his jaw. He dashed to the window and drew the curtains.

He stammered, "Do...do...do you know whatcha saying? The white folks 'round these parts ain't whatcha call respectable. They mad the South loss, and some of 'em still got slaves."

"My mother was a slave. I know what that means."

Clyde stabbed a finger in her face. "If'n you ain't ever been a slave, then you cain't know what it means!"

Rage, fear, and bitterness contorted his features. Tears gushed from his eyes and ran down his face.

He continued lashing out. "You don't know what nuthin' means! If'n you ain't feel the whip, then you don't know shit!!"

Unruffled by his outbursts, she said, "You're right. Do you want me to leave?"

It was a calculated question because she only guessed his loneliness and his longing.

He rubbed his hands on the sides of his pants as he considered. Then he said, "I might be able to git rid of Bailey, say he wandered here cuz I shoed him regular enough—are you sure Ol' John Colby is dead?"

Again, she smiled, "Gutted him myself. Cut his body into pieces. For the wolves."

His eyes widened, then he laughed until he realized he hooted alone. Then, suddenly, with a sweeping glance, he took her in all at once: the long dark hair under the cowboy hat, the man's shirt, and pants, the shooters slung from holsters on her hips, the boots with the glint from a nearly hidden knife tucked inside.

"What's yo name, girl?" He asked, folding his arms and keeping his distance.

In a voice as cold as the snow-capped mountains, she said, "I can't keep my child."

At that, Clyde took a seat. His attention turned to the sleeping babe in her arm.

"Is there anyone in this town who will take in a newly born child?" she asked.

By now, he was sweating. He poured himself a cup of water and drank deep long gulps. His Adam's Apple bobbed as he swigged.

Next, he got up from his seat and went inside the other room. He returned with a liquor bottle, filled the cup, and drank. Then, silently, he offered a swig to Sara, who declined by shaking her head.

He said, "Negro folks live jist a ways off the main stretch. Houses ain't much to look at, but we got a nice church. We is good Christians, and we got us a good preacher, too. I knowed his wife cain't have any chil'uns. If'n that's what you want to do?"

Christians? Her mother had spoken of Christians, but a hawkish spit usually followed the word. Ruthie had only believed in the African God, Obatala. And her shaman father? He used to profess his undying devotion to the Great Spirit. And herself?

Sara believed in darkness.

Her squinting gaze drifted from the black-skinned and handsome Clyde, who watched her wholly with apparent adoration, to the peacefully sleeping babe who hadn't given her a lick of trouble since her birth.

Sara swallowed hard at the decision.

Perhaps seeing her quiet turmoil, Clyde said, "Ain't nuthin you need to decide now. But the sooner, the better, 'specially since I gotta do something with Bailey. Cain't have too much change around us. Make white folks antsy, and they start killin' just to be killin' 'round these parts."

His fear was as palpable as the sweat forming above his thick eyebrows.

Sara remembered the crisscross-raised marks on her mother's back and the frightful ways Ruthie had behaved whenever Sara disappeared from her sight too long. Christians had done that to her mother. They had broken her body, twisted her mind, and taken her children.

"These is Negro Christians," Clyde said as if reading her hesitation. "These is good people. I can tell them a customer was riding through and left dey kid behind. A lot of riffraff do come through here."

Sara tucked No-Name on the bed, wrapped herself around the tiny form, and kissed her forehead. Despair shot ripples throughout her body. She raised her head above the dingy pillow and said, without an ounce of passion, "If anything happens to my child or my horse while I sleep, I will kill you."

He grinned. "You something else. Know that? If you ain't gonna tell me your name, what's the baby's name then?"

She kissed the tip of her child's nose and smelled the sweet aroma of breast milk on her breath.

"Her name is Little Ruthie. My name is Raven, but you can call me Sara."

Clyde said, "Raven? Ruth is a nice Christian name."

Sara rested her head on the pillow and was instantly asleep.

7. STOLEN

SAMMY

• • • •

SAMMY, LEGS IN STIRRUPS, tired from the push, push, pushing, and dizzy from the epidural, couldn't wait to hold her squirming babe.

She grinned at how he resembled a withered old man as the nurse began carting him away.

"I want to hold him," she whispered.

"Soon," a nurse, or was it the doctor, said and patted her hand. Her hunger for contact with her child was intense. Instead of canoodling with the new being, she was cleaned up and then rolled into a private room. Sammy became antsy as time passed. She rang for a nurse in fifteen, then in five-minute intervals. They always appeared without her baby, and she listened as they plied her lie upon lie.

He's being weighed.

He's being fed.

He's still being tested.

We have to wait for the doctor to give him a clean bill of health.

Lies!

Later, her well-groomed father showed up attired in a designer suit. His rich scent hinted at an expensive cologne and ultimate success. Once he arrived, he lingered next to the door as if readying himself for a hasty escape.

"Hi, Dad," she raised on her elbows.

"I have something I need to say. The boy—"

She squinted, immediately suspicious. "You mean my son, Trevor?"

He continued speaking as if her words were meaningless, "Once you told your mother and me that you wanted to put the child up for adoption, I believe that is still the best solution."

Adoption?

She struck the bed with balled fists. "What! Where is my son!"

Perhaps early in her pregnancy, she had mumbled that word, but...no, of course, she couldn't give up her child!

"Where is Trevor!" she demanded, over and again, like a record player with its needle caught in the groove of an old vinyl.

Her heart flipped in her chest with the realization little Trevor was gone. From her. Forever.

Not if she could find him.

She bolted for the door, but she was slow. The whole childbirth thing made her weak. Her dad caught her, and the pair wrestled. She was strong enough to elbow his ribcage, then she used the heel of her hand and slammed it into his nose. Blood sprayed from the injury and onto his tailored clothing. Once he doubled over, she drove her elbow into his spine. He went down with a howl.

Suddenly there were others in the room.

"Where's my son!"

Someone grabbed her hair while another jabbed a needle in her arm. She collapsed at once. Worse, she imagined hearing her sweet child crying out for her rescue.

Her eyelids turned weighty.

"Daddy, please," she murmured. Then darkness lapped over her corneas.

• • • •

SAMMY SANK INTO DARK despondency. After her loss, she'd become little more than a lump of flesh. She refused to eat, walk or care about her appearance. After repeated threats to do so, the hospital staff fed her intravenously. And after a few bowel incidents, they stuffed her in diapers. She felt like she had landed in Dante's Seventh Circle of Hell. What did she expect? Hell was an appropriate place for a murderer, after all.

Trevor was gone. How many months had it been since he was stolen? Two or three? She wasn't sure. She wasn't sure of anything anymore.

Eventually, she was shipped from Brightside to Summerhill, a wholly different psychiatric facility. Instead of living among troubled teens, she was trapped with crazy-as-hell adults.

She missed Brightside. Odd thinking such a thing after the nightmare she'd endured. But the new facility was worse by implementing more controls and fewer options for unrestricted movement. The patients, when not locked in their rooms, were escorted every *damn* where.

Her shroud of despondency briefly lifted one autumn morning. Someone had wheeled her into the crowded Rec Room and positioned her next to the window. The bleak sky drew her attention. Thick clouds rolled across the horizon, and soon after, droplets pelted the window. She hoped the storm was God's way of showing His sympathy for her lost soul. At least He could cry in her stead. She had no more tears to give.

Her agony exploded whenever she tried firmly grasp her golden memory of Trevor. She had wanted so badly to hold him. Oh, and the way he had screamed! She remembered admiring how his prolonged cries announced his presence to the world.

A single thought taunted her with guilt. *What kind of mother forgets the face of her child?*

Tears cascaded down her cheeks. It was a fact that she had forgotten the nuances of his features. Now, she only saw his face as an ill-defined abstract. She was hopeless, and living was useless.

A flash of lightning brightened the Rec room and jolted Sammy from her suicidal thoughts. Then, an instant later, thunder boomed and set off an array of inhuman noises from the frantic inmates.

Sammy whimpered while the outer storm paralleled her inner agony.

"Trevor," she mouthed his name.

Once again, thunder rumbled overhead. Several of the spooked patients made frightful, repetitive commotions. A young woman near the door began beating her head with a balled fist while laughing hysterically. A gangly man pitched individual playing cards at the window as he sang the Star-Spangled Banner. An orderly chased another man who dropped his pants and waved his dangling penis at the other residents like a sword.

The low crescendo of lunacy heightened each time thunder rumbled or lighting flashed. Soon after, the orderlies marshaled the residents out of the Rec Room.

Since she appeared to be a soulless body, she was the last one hustled into the poorly lit and narrow hall. From the looks of them, the meager staff was bottom-barrel and, to her limited experience, slovenly trained. The orderly rolling her to her cramped room was a skinny dullard. But, given his musty body odor, he was also allergic to soap.

She was roughly lifted and then dumped onto her bed. He locked her inside with only her recriminations for company. The storm moved on, and moonlight stuffed every crevice with shadows. Later, a nurse appeared, inserted an intravenous tube, and checked her vitals. No one changed her diaper, and Sammy slept in her filth.

She had a rash and suffered from bedsores. Meanwhile, her weight dropped until she was less than one hundred pounds. Most of all, she just wanted to die.

8. THE STUUMI IN NYSA

*****SAMMY*****

••••

A GIGANTIC CIRCULAR lamp hovered over her head. Sammy studied the disc without an expression and stared directly into the light without much blinking. Neither was she alarmed by the straps securing her arms and legs to the examination table.

Nothing mattered.

Dr. Gibson was a petite man with squinty eyes. He had a deformed right ear that was pointy and hung lower than the other. Behind his back, she'd heard the staff call him Satan.

His attempt at a smile revealed stained teeth and an overbite. His efforts at openness never felt genuine. She wouldn't trust him to butter bread.

"No need to be alarmed, Samantha." He wheezed in her face.

Ah, yes, she thought. *Halitosis.*

He continued, "We've talked about giving you an ECT if your depression didn't alleviate. Shock therapy has a bad reputation. All I'm going to do is give you a brief mild seizure. It will only last a minute."

He caressed Sammy's head in a grandfatherly fashion. "Therapy isn't working. Drugs aren't working. We need you to come back to us."

Nysa, she thought. *Nysa, Nysa, Nysa. Now I remember Nysa. I want to go to Nysa. Nysa, Nysa, Nysa.*

"I'm going to give you something to help you sleep." He made a two-fingered motion to the anesthesiologist. The androgynous young woman responded with a subtle nod.

Dr. Gibson continued, "We'll also give you a muscle relaxant."

The mickey was injected into the iv-tubing protruding from her hand while electrodes were taped to the shaved parts of her scalp.

Sammy glanced at the nearby machine purring to life. It seemed innocuous enough, resembling an old-fashioned radio box or a laptop computer. Thin white paper, charted with zig-zag black lines, spat from the mouth of the apparatus.

She didn't want an ECT. She didn't want them to reset her brain.

A kind voice floated from another plane of existence and urged her to count backward from one hundred.

Sammy refused and swore that she would never, ever speak again.

• • • •

NYSA.

Paradise was under assault by a blustery storm. The rolling black clouds produced an incessant downpour as trees bowed in a howling gale.

The irony of her predicament wasn't elusive. Sammy had at long last reached utopia, the sanctuary she had craved, only to find Nysa in turmoil, just like her soul.

She stood on the cliff overlooking the waterfall as rain pelted her skin. She couldn't ignore the immediate yearning in her heart.

Where the hell is Sara?

When was the last time they had met in paradise? Ages ago. Just the thought of her twin impaled her with sharp stabs to the heart.

She dropped to her knees, and mud slopped over her skin. She was somewhat alarmed to see how even in Eden, she wore the paper-thin hospital gown. Her fingernails, once proudly manicured, were ragged. The pigment underneath was grey from medication. She dug her nails into the earth and screamed until her rage subsided as if it had never existed.

As she tilted her face to the sky, the rain washed over her features. Was God weeping for her lost soul? Or was she losing herself here, as well?

Better in here than out there, she thought.

She crawled, on hands and knees, to the cliff's edge and peered down at the raging waters. She was mesmerized by the spraying foamy geysers churning between large boulders.

She rolled back until her bottom touched her heels and smothered an odd sensation as she watched the splattering water burst on the rocks. Again she examined her hand, but this time she noticed the transparency of her flesh. If she concentrated, she could see beyond her cocoa-hued skin right through pink meat, sinewy tendons, and bones. Was she fading?

Would death be so bad?

She could do it. She could off herself. All she had to do was save up the horrid combination of daily pharmaceuticals and then gulp them in one sitting. Easy peasy. No problemo. After all, she wasn't immortal like Sara. She could die.

At once, the wind quieted as if Nysa heard her melancholy thoughts.

She heard a woman's faint whimpers from somewhere close. The moans erupted into unsettling shrieks. Sammy listened as the melancholy sounds died, only to restart louder and longer.

Timidly, Sammy shouted, "Sara, is that you?"

Somehow, she knew the hideous sounds couldn't come from her twin. Besides, the jarring cries seemed too bizarre to be human.

A wounded animal? In Nysa? Of course not! There was no pain in paradise.

As the distressing noises continued to ebb and then swell, Sammy wondered what kind and how many animals suffered in severe pain. Then her thoughts became more frightening. What if the hair-raising sounds wailed from a single throat?

Although fearful, she craned her neck to pinpoint the source or sources. Then she spotted a light in the woods. The glow flickered some distance away like a bad omen. Mesmerized, Sammy found herself walking toward it against her will. She even tried digging her naked toes first in mud and then in the grass.

Finally, she reached a clearing where a strange sight forced her to clamp a hand over her mouth. She stifled the scream but not the shock.

A naked and charred creature writhed in a jerky dance as if in perpetual pain. The thing had the form of an athletic young woman whose burnt epidermis revealed patches of bloodless meat. The light source Sammy had tracked, against her will, came from the bluish fire ringing the creature's bald head. Her features were shriveled, just patches of black flesh pasted on a gleaming white skull. What horrified Sammy most were the hellion's eyes. Fire jettisoned from the sockets each time she moved, no matter how minuscule the action.

Sammy halted her zombie-like movements a few feet from the she-thing.

The scabby wraith stopped her erratic dance and quieted her unearthly howling once the pair were face-to-face.

A ragged voice resounded in Sammy's mind, *"Your pain called me. Do you want to die? Is that why I'm here?"*

"Who the hell are you," she whispered with fear trembling her words.

Though fire spewed from the pits where her eyes should've been, tears steamed and sizzled down the being's shriveled cheeks.

"Sammy, you are stronger than Sara. You want to live. I know you do." Then she opened her mouth, allowing a cacophony of chilling swinish-like sounds to escape.

Sammy clamped her hands over her ears and screamed, "Stop it! You sound like the fucking Exorcist or something!" Although repelled by the nightmarish howl, Sammy had to ask, "How do you know my name?"

The ghostlike wails continued until Sammy endured a blast of heat from the beastie's cavernous mouth. The raw sewage stench was horrific.

Sammy had no desire to flee because she had no fight left in her soul.

In the real world, there were pills, shock treatments, and talk—talk—talk, but she was home now. She was in Nysa. But more than being home, she felt a bit of understanding developing in her muddled brain.

The creature tilted her head as if rummaging through Sammy's thoughts.

"Got it!" Sammy snapped her fingers." I do know who you are! You're Sara's trickster. You're the Stuuwi, aren't you? Damn! No wonder she's afraid of you."

"I'm no trickster. She's the trickster. She's the one who can't see her power. I'm the only one who is aware."

The word, *aware*, lingered in Sammy's mind. The long, harsh whisper of it forced Sammy to take a fright-filled involuntary backward step.

"I want to help you too."

"Help me? How can you help me?"

Suddenly, Sammy had a scarier thought. What if she wasn't in Nysa? What if she was tripping on a bad batch of meds? Dr. Gibson was a bullet-head, and screwing up her drugs was entirely possible?

Sammy, now truly defiant, shouted, "Okay then. Since you want to help, go away! I bet I created you from Sara's description! You're her nightmare, not mine! You're not real! I said, go away!"

The Stuuwi didn't move. Instead, the flames lapping her skull brightened. Sammy shielded herself from the light by hiding behind her hands. And she heard the creature sobbing.

Sammy cursed her foolhardiness. She had believed what her eyes revealed as fact, that she was in the company of a monster, but now her heart told her that she had it all wrong.

Stuuwi continued wailing as her thoughts continued invading Sammy's mind, "*Do you think you know everything, too? Like her? You both know nothing. You both want to feel nothing. You treat me like I'm nothing. Why do you ignore my help? Why do you hurt me?"*

Sammy awakened to the fading echoes of the Stuuwi's heartbreaking sobs.

"I'm sorry," she murmured. For the first time in a long time, real tears dampened her face. "I was a real bitch to you. I'm so sorry. And you're right. I do want to live. Thank you, Stuuwi, for showing me that I'm still human. That I still have a heart."

COLD-BLOODED RINGERS

9. A BREATH OF CAMILA

SAMMY

• • • •

SAMMY PUKED IN THE aluminum pan and slid it on the nightstand without spilling the contents. Unless a nurse collected her upchuck, she would have to smell the crap all night long.

She wiped a thin line of drool from her chin and reclined, exhausted, on the pillow. Her stomach rioted, and before she could coalesce a coherent thought, she snatched the pan from the tiny table and hacked up another bucketload of bile.

She considered her persistent nausea as the worst of the ECT side effects. At least the shock therapy sessions lifted the crippling veil of dissociation and muted the pain of her maternal loss. She knew she'd given a child up for adoption, but now she couldn't remember giving birth or what he looked like, which was worrisome. The absence of his being should matter.

A knock on her door disrupted her thoughts. The orderly, a thick matron with a menopausal mustache, shuffled into the room.

"Dinner time?" she wondered. Although, by her tone, it was clear Sammy wasn't given an option.

Nevertheless, Sammy shook her head. "I can't eat."

The woman crossed her meaty arms as she sneered at the challenge.

Sammy didn't want to fight. Instead, she placed her puke pan back on the night table and followed the woman to the Rec Room, where the kitchen staff served their food.

She stood in line, wobbling a bit, and retrieved a plastic tray and utensils. She collected the offered plate of a meatloaf-like substance and grimaced while her stomach roiled. She walked, weak-kneed, to the nearest table and sat closest to the window.

She looked for Zeus. She couldn't help herself. But her wolfdog was obedient, which meant he wasn't there. He probably thought she was still at Brightside.

She shuddered. Summerhill was so bad that she missed Brightside. Then, as she stirred a lumpy mixture passing for mashed potatoes, she wondered how things could've gotten so bad that she longed for that hellhole.

A diminutive girl dropped her tray on the table and sat, uninvited, across from Sammy. "Hey, you woke up?" she asked in a cheery voice and began shoveling food into her mouth.

Sammy recoiled at the intrusion and immediately sought an unoccupied table. But they were all taken.

The young Latina was beautiful. She had a baby face, and her dark hair was pulled back into a cute ponytail. She batted her long eyelashes in a faux innocent manner and asked, "Whatcha looking for?"

"Privacy," Sammy retorted. "I guess it ain't happening now," she whispered.

"I didn't think you would mind some company," the girl said, unfazed by Sammy's standoffishness. She extended her hand. "Camila."

"Sammy." She lifted an eyebrow without accepting the invitation.

"Shit, everybody knows who you is." She pointed her index finger like a gun. "Pow, pow. Shot those sons of bitches dead in that rich bitch private school. They thought they were gonna be all gangsta with their shit, but you took out those white niggers like fucking Rambo. You got like a gazillion likes on Facebook. Glad they put me in here with you."

The memory of that incident returned to bite her, and she groaned. Then, quickly, she said, "Not proud of killing them. You must be new?"

Camila tore off a bit of dry bread and dunked it into the pretend gravy, and ate with relish.

"I ain't new. Been talking to you for months," she said.

Months?

Sammy was startled. She didn't know if she should've been embarrassed or saddened. Instead, she cleared her throat and asked, "What have you been saying?"

"This and that, mostly about this place."

The girl's lack of manners repulsed Sammy. Camila spoke too fast despite having a mouth full of food. Every so often, pasty bits sprayed over her plate.

Sammy pushed aside her tray.

"You not go eat that?"

Sammy swallowed the urge to barf. She pressed her hand to her lips and shook her head.

"You ain't gonna throw up, are you?"

"No," she whispered, although she wasn't sure. She willed Camila to stop talking. But it didn't work.

Camila scooped in another mouthful of food, reached across the table, and helped herself to Sammy's bread. Then, as she chomped off a piece and chewed, she eyed her tablemate.

Sammy was ready to leave.

"Got leaked out you got raped in Brightside. Man, you are a media darling. You should do a podcast. You could make a lot of money. Well, except we're in here."

"What?" Sammy pressed a hand on her abdomen. "The whole world knows about that?"

Camila regarded Sammy as if she were an imbecile. "Well, duh. Ain't lying to you. They DNA'd the dead dude and, sure enough, him the daddy. You really rich now. They had to close Brightside because your lawsuit helped to wipe them out. Didn't you know that?"

Sammy wanted her to stop talking. But her heart raced as she heard herself ask. "I didn't dream it? He's really dead?"

Camila looked furtively around to see if their conversation was being overheard, then she leaned in close. "Dang girl, ain't nobody telling you nuthin'? I got this 4-1-1 from your rich boyfriend before I got pinched. Now I have to earn my computer privileges. Muthafuckers! Anyway, he's been plastering all kinds of shit on Facebook. Dude's in love with you."

Sammy asked again, this time through clenched teeth, "He's really dead?"

"Who? Baby's daddy? Found him all chewed up on his front porch. You had a dog, didn't you?" Camila raised a suspicious eyebrow, and the action made her appear endearing.

Sammy looked out the window.

Zeus?

Frightened, Sammy asked, "Did they catch the dog?"

"Huh?"

She hadn't been in contact with Zeus since forever! She was on her feet, trembling with fear. Had he been put down? Was that why she hadn't seen him?

Sammy screamed, "The dog, Camila! What about the damn dog!"

A matron hustled to the table and grabbed Sammy's arm. She freed herself with a jerk. The woman quickly motioned to an orderly, a rough-looking giant who donned a no-nonsense attitude as he approached.

Sammy thought about it. A punch to the woman's gut and a knee to the man's groin, but she was too nauseous to fight. Besides, she was ninety-eight pounds of ashy skin and brittle bones. And honestly, what was the point?

"Calm down," Camila said as she picked up her tray. "Dog's all right. He's living with somebody named Marsha, I think." Then she hurried to an empty seat at another table.

The chunky matron grabbed one arm while the brute seized the other. Sammy didn't notice the less-than-delicate handling.

She only thought about her baffling conversation with Camila. How did she know about Marsha? And she prayed Zeus was safe! The first moment she had alone, she would try to link with him.

Sammy was roughly hoisted from her seat and half-dragged through the double-door exit. She looked over her shoulder at Camila. The young girl, still eating, winked and then stood up. She cupped her mouth and blasted loudly, "Sara's real, by the way." Her shout instigated animated chatters in the room.

Another orderly threatened, "Sit down and shut up!"

She knows about Sara?

The automatic door slammed shut, but it didn't matter. Sammy's bewildered heart threatened to crack a rib.

How would she know? Maybe I spoke about her while my mind was gone bye-bye?

Of course, there was the likelihood Camila had snooped into Sammy's files somehow, but what if she hadn't? Sammy sensed Camila was an old soul. She didn't think she was wrong about that. What if *old soul* meant gifted, special, or—what was the word—was it clairvoyant?

For the first time in a long time, she smiled.

10. A FRIEND IN HELL

SARA

• • • •

MILLER'S TOWN SPRANG into existence when the Miller boys, deserters from the Confederacy, tapped a silver vein in one of the nearby mines. Their prospecting enriched the former Southern farmers and made the papers, thus turning their little stretch of land into a full-fledged town.

In truth, only the Millers knew the site of their particular ore-rich mine. It was equally valid that they had hacked out the last bit of silver after only a few months. But that didn't stop the hopefuls from arriving, building homes, and staking claims on worthless pits.

The town was close to a natural water source. Although the winters were harsh, the growing season was decent for crops and livestock. And the view of the mountains was picturesque.

Newcomers seeking their fortune arrived initially by stagecoach. Since locomotives needed water for steam, the town was an ideal whistle-stop, so the railroad followed suit until the community of a few hundred swelled to over one thousand. Progress came with the homesteaders. Miller's Town boasted a dry goods store, a telegraph office, a post office, and a saloon housing a brothel on the second floor. Homes lined the main street. And in the center of the bustling area were the Sheriff's office and jail.

On the outskirts of the main town was a smaller community, Darkie Town, where the homes were little more than shacks. Some of the colored inhabitants were farmers, while a few worked in Miller's Town as stock clerks, handymen, or maids. Others hired themselves out as ranch hands. The only Negro business within the main town belonged to Clyde Washington. His smithing skills earned him some measure of respect. But not much.

Miller's Town had Southern roots. The townsfolk, mainly the settlers, professed Christianity, yet their religion lacked brotherly love.

Sara, who had grown up as an outcast in her village, was schooled on a different kind of oppression. In this new community, hatred proved to be deadly. A simple social offense could easily result in a lynching. It was hard for her to understand she was dehumanized solely because of her complexion. But skin color meant everything, and hers implied she was a promiscuous beast only worthy of scorn.

Sometimes she forgot her place, but a deft shove or a wad of spit were excellent reminders. She learned how to move and behave. So yes, she kept her head down, and her eyes lowered. She shifted aside on the wooden sidewalks for the white folks, even if it meant stepping into a pile of horseshit. She stood in line at the General Store, often losing her turn to newly entering white customers and holding her tongue when she was charged twice as much for the same goods. For the time being, there was little she could do or say to change her circumstances. All she could do was endure.

There was a bright spot in her life.

Clyde had given Little Ruthie to the preacher and his wife. He had promised they were good Christian people as if she fully understood what his claim meant. But without her child, her intolerable situation had worsened.

Again, what were her other choices? None. She was incapable of mothering. Yet, after Little Ruthie was gone, she languished in a deep well of self-pity for months.

Eventually, Clyde encouraged her to live and schooled her on acceptable behaviors. She learned, in his cramped living quarters, how to breathe again. Although her benefactor gave much of himself, she found his world was too antagonistic for her comfort.

She was worried, too. After all, she had killed John Colby, a white man. But mountain men lived on the fringes of society. If folks bothered to care, they assumed he had just taken off. Some layabouts hanging around the shop often lamented how he'd skipped out owing them money.

And Bailey? Clyde had sold him to a stranger passing through town.

So maybe she was safe after all.

Life continued under the ever-present oppression that folded around her like a veil. She had little choice but to assimilate completely. So she wore those awful long dresses with undergarments, which bound her movements to small, inconsequential actions.

Because the dry season produced high winds that generated dust and tumbleweeds, she wore bonnets to protect her hair. When she realized her long dark hair drew unwanted attention, she braided her tresses and rolled the plaits into a bun.

Her shoes, which had low heels, weren't suitable for running or performing laborious chores. Plus, they squeezed and pinched her toes.

The tight-fitting attire caused her to sweat profusely, which was against one of Sammy's main rules, *don't let them smell you coming.*

Remembering Sammy and her rules—*keep your teeth clean* or *bathe on the regular*—often forced Sara to smile. But given her circumstances, the modest act didn't last long. At least Sammy would've appreciated how hard she was trying.

On Sundays, she attended service with Clyde. A week's worth of black repression was let loose in the church where a plump man preached, and the choir sang joyful gospel music. The brightly dressed Baptists danced and hollered in the name of Gawd.

Their revelry reminded her of the lively village ceremonies that worshipped Nesharu and Mother Corn in the Medicine Lodge.

Sara had no use for religion. Nesharu hadn't protected His people. And despite all the praising and hoopla, Gawd wasn't protecting His people either. The gods were deaf or dead.

The real reason she faithfully attended was so that she could glimpse her Little Ruthie. The babe was now a toddler. And she was beautiful and well-mannered. She and Clyde, the blacksmith and his assumed mail-order bride from Kentucky, were regulars. They usually sat near the rear, where Sara could quietly observe her baby without drawing unwarranted attention.

The first time she attended, with her arm linked with Clyde's, whispers swirled around them before they sat on the wooden pews.

The preacher took one look at Sara, mopped his sweating face, and side-eyed the bundle squirming in his wife's arms. Although the woman's back was to her, Sara saw the preacher's wife stiffen in her seat.

Clyde squeezed her hand while Sara closed her eyes and pretended to pray. The agony was bearable because Little Ruthie was clean, dressed in fine clothing, and appeared well-fed. And during those moments when the church was somewhat quiet, she could be heard cooing.

Later, her child always seemed content whenever Sara saw the preacher and his family in Darkie Town. His wife often held the babe tighter, and they avoided Sara by crossing the dusty street or ducking into a store.

Then one Sunday, it was all undone when a new preacher delivered the sermon from the pulpit. He was a firebrand who energized the congregation.

Sara was horrified.

Where was the old preacher? His wife?

More importantly, where was her daughter!

Only Clyde's soothing words and his promise to investigate kept her from a screaming fit.

After the service, Clyde chatted with a withered church elder. Too fidgety but appearing calm, Sara forced herself to wait until the men ended their conversation by standing some distance and staring at a tree. At the end of their talk, Clyde joined her under the tree's shade. His forlorn expression amplified her anxiety.

"C'mon. I'll tell ya when we git home." Then he took her hand. She agreed. He only shared his information after downing a shot of whiskey.

"Them moved to California. He got a job waiting for them out there. They been trying to leave town for months. When the new preacher done come, they packed up and left—left like thieves in the night. Didn't leave no forwarding address. That's what the old deacon said."

Little Ruthie is gone? Forever?

Her existence felt more abrasive, and the need to assimilate peeled off her psyche like the skin of a rotting banana.

While in town, she provoked with her direct eye-to-eye contact, and she never gave deference by stepping off the sidewalk.

She barged into shops, insisted on making her purchases whenever she was ready, and denounced clerks as swindling cheats whenever they doubled their prices on her items because she hated everyone.

And poor Clyde. She detested his subservience. He was a giant who wielded his tools with unfathomable strength, yet he cowered around whites like a beaten dog. Suddenly their unity became toxic. Her love-making turned punitive, with slaps, pokes, and bites.

He didn't complain. Obviously, he loved Sara and tried to soothe her maternal pain with patient gentleness.

Sara wouldn't have any of his warmth or understanding. Men didn't know. How could they?

She was ready to leave. But to where? She didn't have a destination in mind, or did she? California? She didn't know where it was, and her decision to leave without a plan was foolhardy, but she couldn't stay in Miller's Town any longer.

That's what she told herself. But in truth, she was trapped. Sara had no money and no place to go. So she swept Clyde's house clean, prepared his meals, and kept his bed warm while she died just a little bit each day.

• • • •

THE AFTERNOON WAS HOT. A year had elapsed since the preacher, and his wife had taken her daughter to California. Although she didn't think she could, somehow, Sara adapted.

One afternoon, as she contemplated her hatred of Miller's Town, she passed the saloon. Despite the early hour and above the gamblers' jabberings, she heard nimble fingers playing the piano.

According to the hotheaded preacher, saloons were no place for decent Christian folk. Even Negroes crossed the street to avoid contact with the heathens patronizing the vulgar establishment. She never forgot how John Colby had almost lured her into prostitution. She remembered his deception often as she walked the wooden planks outside the whiskey establishment. And today was no exception as she toted a bag of wrapped buffalo meat. Yet, this time, as sweat dotted her forehead, she stopped.

A cool breeze swept over the saloon's swinging doors, giving her a soothing chill. Curious, she dared look inside.

She saw men seated at green-covered round tables playing cards while a rotund man with a bristly mustache sat at a marred piano and nimbly stroked the keys into a rousing melody.

A young woman with tight blonde ringlets piled high atop her head appeared.

She gave Sara a rouge-colored smile and joined her on the sidewalk. "Hey you," she asked, "you wanna come in?"

She was pretty, older than Sara by about five years, and she stood half an inch taller. The woman smelled sweet, like rose petals, and her lavender dress shimmered from shiny beads.

Sara took a hesitant backward step. But she didn't avoid eye contact. Instead, she kept her head held high and smirked.

The woman extended her hand, "Name's Violet."

"Raven." She grasped the hand warmly and shook.

Violet opened the swinging salon door and said, "Come inside and have a drink."

"I don't drink," Sara said. Then she heard the eerie quiet, and after peering once again inside the saloon, she saw how the card games and the piano playing had halted.

"I can't."

Violet turned back to the saloon and waved her hand. The card and music playing resumed.

She said, "Pay them no attention. This is my establishment. Plus, my man is almost as big as yours."

Violet then slightly inclined her head to the large, bald man behind the bar. She continued, "Pussy pays better than the mines. I run most of this town because I own most of the buildings."

Sara liked her frankness.

Violet eyed the package leaking blood, and then her inquisitive stare returned to Sara's face. Her pouty lips lifted into a winsome smile. "You're different. You can read. I saw you reading a Wanted poster. Don't you know you're not supposed to read? At least in public?"

"And?"

Violet's laughter was boisterous and infectious.

Sara noticed how passersby gave them a wide berth, including whites, but some also tilted their hats as a sign of respect.

"I think we're beginning to understand each other," she said, toying with a freed strand of Sara's dark hair. "You're so pretty."

"I'm not a whore," Sara said frankly.

Violet smiled, "No, you're much more than that. You move like a gunslinger. There's something dark behind your eyes. You have the eyes of a killer. Cold. Even though you pretend, I see bad things when I see you."

It was Sara's turn to analyze. "You were attacked when you were young. You were raped and deserted and hurt. You hate being a woman because it makes you feel weak. And you're ashamed you have to use other women to survive." Sara retrieved the strand and tucked it behind her ear.

"I treat my girls kindly. I don't beat them, and I don't cheat them. They've already suffered rough lives. I give them a chance to earn money and to save it." Then she said, "You shouldn't talk to me this way."

Sara smirked. "I have a few minutes. I think I'll have that drink now."

The saloon's interior was dark and cool. Violet's man sprang from his post and took Sara's package. He had a menacing scar descending from his left eye to the left corner of his mouth. His green eyes sparkled as he winked at Violet, who then kissed him tenderly.

"Thank you, Charlie. Tuck that in the meat safe until Raven leaves," she cooed, leaving a bright red lipstick stain on his lips. "Bring us a bottle of the good stuff. We're going to have a girl chat."

With his free hand, Charlie wiped the bar once, threw the towel over his left shoulder, and then departed to a back room.

Sara followed Violet to the farthest table in the saloon, where she took a seat and marveled at the comfortable cushion fixed in the chair.

There were less than fifteen patrons. Most were crusty young men in cowboy chaps. One look at Sara had some flinging their cards on the playing tables, cursing. Several prepared to exit.

"Now, now, friends," Violet chastised in a sing-song voice. "Just remember, if you walk out that door, you don't get to come back to my wonderful establishment."

Most awkwardly returned to their tables, mumbling under their breaths. But a cranky old-timer with wiry sideburns refused to stay. Instead, he spat as he headed for the door, "Don't cotton to anybody treatin' niggers like regular folks. Ain't natural."

"Sorry you feel that way," Violet retorted. "Make sure you pay your tab in full on your way out."

He stomped as he protested, "C'mon, Miss Violet! You know I ain't got that kind of money until the end of the month. This ain't right, and you knowed it!"

She held out her palm for payment, and her fingernails were long and pointy.

Charlie returned with the good stuff. By now, his scowl was nearly lethal.

The old-timer gulped and grumbled before shuffling back to his table and joining his cohorts.

Sara asked, "What if they tell the sheriff?"

Violet's laughter was light and hearty. "I told you. My town, my sheriff. He gets paid too."

Charlie placed the bottle and two shot glasses on the table, then returned to the business side of the bar.

Violet poured their drinks, raised a glass, and held it up. She gave Sara a quizzical look before laughing again. "I'm waiting for you to do the same."

When Sara obliged, Violet clinked their glasses. "Cheers." She drained her glass and made a face.

Sara did the same, only she made an open mouth, tongue stuck out, face as the bitter liquid burned down her throat.

"Good, huh?" Violet said and poured them another drink.

"Real good," Sara remarked.

Violet asked, "Do you know what an enigma is?"

Sara shook her head but stopped quickly because the action caused the room to spin. She liked the floating feeling and lightheadedness and indicated she wanted another drink, which she gulped with gusto.

"Neither did I, but I had a customer, an educated man who loved to talk. I learned a lot from him, but that was before Charlie." And she raised her glass to honor the bartender mopping up a fresh spill from a teetotaler occupying a stool.

Violet continued, "You're a mystery. Right now, you should be good and drunk, so maybe I will get the truth?" She leaned in close and whispered, "You've got a good man. Clyde knows how to play ignorant, but he's also a good fuck."

Sara was startled, and unfortunately, the drink made her show it. "What do you want to know?" she asked, her words slurring.

"Honestly, I'm curious. Clyde made up some story when he sold Bailey to a customer. Then I see you trouncing around town at the same time the Negro preacher and his wife get a half-white baby girl wearing a strange necklace. I hear you have one exactly like it under that dress. Tongues wag in small towns, don't you know."

This time Sara poured herself another drink and downed it without taking her eyes off Violet.

"What's your question?" Sara asked.

"John's place was burned down to the ground. The sheriff questioned me about a customer seen riding Bailey out of town." When Sara screwed in her face, Violet added, "Don't worry, I left Clyde out of it."

Sara expelled a breath, surprised that she had been holding it.

"What happened in those mountains between you and John? Is that his baby?"

"Rape."

Sara poured the last bit of whiskey into her glass. It meant her death if she admitted to killing a white man. She swished the drink in her mouth with absolute delight and savored the heady effects. Yet her smile was crooked and menacing.

Violet slightly recoiled and then leaned in again to whisper. "Dark and evil behind those eyes. It's enticing. I have some advice. Why don't you take your beautiful black horse and ride the hell out of this town? I don't want you to go, but you must get as far away as possible from Miller's Town and any place like it."

Sara reached across the table and placed her hand over Violet's. The other woman interlocked their fingers.

Sara admitted, "You're right because I'm dying here."

Charlie brought them another bottle and poured their drinks.

Violet raised her glass.

Sara followed suit.

This time, when their glasses clinked, Violet toasted, "To a new lifelong friend."

11. UNJUST RAGE

SARA

• • • •

AN UNRULY COMMOTION seeped through the stone walls of their living area. The din was so loud it clamored above Clyde's consistent hammering. She heard as he abruptly stopped striking heavy metal on the anvil.

He rushed, openly alarmed, into their living quarters, where Sara lounged on the bed, perusing a tattered paper. His expressions wavered from fear to anger and back to fear. She scowled as she folded the paper and stuffed it under the mattress.

"What? Nobody can see me reading."

Then she absorbed the angry voices punctuated with taunting yet cheerless laughter. She had lived in Miller's Town long enough to understand the insinuations. Her skin crawled at the significance of the sounds.

Clyde's eyes rounded. "Stay here!"

He fled the bedroom. Sara, never mindful, followed as he shut down his business by securing the doors and closing the shutters.

The pair stood still in the darkened room, hugging each other as the frenzied shouts reached a crescendo and then moved beyond their area. Sara tried to make sense of the garbled words. Then, within the massive storm of incoherent fury, she heard a sobbing man begging for help.

She ran to the door when Clyde stopped her by using his body as a barrier. And with tears in his eyes, he said, "Ain't nothing we kin do for him. He a dead man."

Sara bit her lower lip to keep from shouting, and while batting back tears, she asked, "Why? What did he do?"

"Don't matter," Clyde said. "Wrong place at the wrong time 'spose. Like that 'round here."

The raucous jubilation moved further away from the town limits.

Sara whispered, "What about the sheriff?"

His eyes narrowed, and he said gruffly, "He ain't *our* sheriff. 'Sides, he cain't stop no lynch mob."

Sara swept her shawl over her shoulders and met his gaze with her glare until he stepped aside. Then she unbarred the door and slipped out of the shop.

"Cain't help him!" he hissed. "Leave it be!"

Sara lifted the folds of her skirt and ran. Behind her, she heard Clyde shutting and bolting the door. She crouched low and followed the crowd's path outside the town's limits.

She was compelled to see.

The mob's jeering unified next to the dilapidated cemetery populated by crooked headstones and weeds. Sara darted behind a hill but crept closer on her hands and knees.

She watched as a thin, sobbing mulatto, bound with a thick rope around his wrists, was led by one of the men on horseback. The procession stopped at a gigantic black tree with naked, gnarled branches scraping the severe gray sky.

The colored man, encircled by the mocking spectators, bled from cuts to his face and slashed torso. Blood ran from his swollen eyes like tears.

A horseback rider tossed a noose over a thick and twisted branch. A man wearing a badge grabbed the loop and tightened it around the condemned man's neck.

The resulting cheers were deafening.

The rider circled rope around his saddle horn and kicked the steed into motion.

The beaten man was hoisted in a sharp jerk with his bare toes skimming the ground. His eyes rolled backward. His neck bent at a crooked angle as he choked while he kicked wildly.

Some in the swarm of onlookers showered his twitching form with rotted food and spittle. Gradually, the man stopped moving and swayed from the twisted limb like a broken toy.

Soon after, his body was lowered, stripped of his torn and bloody clothing until he was naked, and then some of the men cut pieces of flesh and handed them to the bystanders as tokens.

Sara clasped her mouth and swallowed vomit.

Nearby, women spread out blankets and unloaded wicker baskets of food. The families sat nearby on the grass, some with their children in tow, and had a picnic.

Sara had seen too much. She clawed the impacted earth until her fingernails broke and the nubs bled. Fear and rage churned her intestines, and she wept as she slunk home.

Clyde was pacing outside the shop, and when he saw her, he ran to meet her and held her against his rapidly beating heart.

Sara was too scared to speak. The unabashed hatred in Miller's Town covered her like a blanket. The welts on her mother's back had a new meaning. And again, she thought of her stolen siblings.

She buried her face in the reliable comfort of Clyde's chest. He led her inside their home, closed the door, and held her as fatigue overcame her until she finally drifted into a fright-filled sleep.

12. ERROR IN JUDGEMENT

SARA

• • • •

FREEDOM.

The full moon highlighted the dark prairie landscape where Sara's soul merged with her galloping black steed. Out of sight in the Plains, she rode with wild abandon. Fusing with Midnight redeemed her soul and slackened her emotional bondage.

As the wind whipped her dark hair, she bunched the reins in her fist and whooped her pleasure. Her excitement rolled up from her chest and rang out as full-throated ululations that echoed in the night.

Sara was ecstatic by the sensation of Midnight's heaving between her thighs because their bonding made her feel alive. She savored the sweet sounds of his snorting nostrils as his thunderous hooves trampled with power and vigor.

In the vast emptiness, Sara, clad in a man's shirt, trousers, and heavy boots, prodded Midnight to run harder and faster. With her jet-black hair unfettered and clinging to her neck from sweat, she basked in her solitude.

Finally, she was Raven again.

Midnight charged the terrain with such incredible speed that his hooves seemed to have wings.

After a time, and once they were far enough from town, she halted him. Then, heaving from exertion, she reached inside her saddlebag and retrieved a bottle of amber-colored hooch. She took a long swig. The effects seemed instantaneous. She, in a boisterous manner, toasted Violet's generosity. It was the good stuff.

Finally, after hours of roaming the countryside, she guided Midnight back toward town. She mournfully sighed when the pair reached the outskirts. Then she dismounted, finished the last swallow of whiskey, and tossed the bottle before leading her horse to their home.

By now, she was so drunk she could barely focus. Luckily for her, Midnight entered his stall without too much provocation.

"Thank you," she said as she plucked his towel from the gate and wiped the sweat from his glossy black coat. Yet, the simple task took tremendous concentration in her inebriated state.

"I'll bet you're hungry," she slurred.

She emptied feed into his manger and pumped fresh water into a bucket. But she found her efforts humorous when she slopped some onto the ground.

Exhausted or perhaps too sloshed to stand further, she pressed her back against the wall facing his stall and slid down onto the floor without a measure of grace.

"There," she said with a gregarious puff. "Fed and watered."

Midnight stared at her without batting his long eyelashes as the wave of love emitting from him was intense.

"Me too. You're all I have left," Sara mumbled.

The numbing from the liquor faded when she remembered in gory detail the mulatto's lynching.

Her life as a young outcast in the people's village had been horrible, but living as a Negro in Miller's Town was far worse.

"Bowing and scraping." She slurred, "Move aside, say nothing, eyes downcast. Yes, ma'am. No, sir. All mean the same thing. Don't beat me, don't torture me, or kill me."

She descended into melancholy, and tears streamed down her cheeks before she realized she was crying.

She backhanded her eyes and read Midnight's compassion.

"We can't keep doing this, can we? You and I, we don't belong here, do we? But where would we go? I don't know where to go. Do you?"

He neighed his response as he nodded his long-maned head, jiggling the beads woven close to his neck.

Suddenly images unfurled over her vision, revealing flatlands while she simultaneously tasted an abundance of freedom.

She responded to the pictures by saying, "So you *do* want to leave too?"

Yet, it wasn't that simple. How could Sara make him understand? They needed food and shelter. Yet why shouldn't she consider his idea? After all, she was an accomplished hunter with a bow and arrow, and she could find grass and brush for him.

Her hope deflated. Escape into the Plains without food, water, or a decent plan wouldn't work. They would die out there like her mother almost did.

She rolled her eyes backward and batted her lids as she linked and communicated with him.

Midnight shook his massive head. Soon after, he backed further into his stall and closed his eyes.

The matter wasn't finished.

Still, Sara was too tired to insert her will.

She yawned and stretched before weaving in a drunken stride to the cabin side of the shop. Before she could rap on the door, Clyde threw it open, jerked her inside, and slammed it shut.

"Cain't keep runnin' off like that!" he snapped. He undressed her. She allowed it. Then she fell back on the bed. He covered her with a thin sheet and slid next to her.

"Ain't nuthin' good go happen if you keep going out at night," he said.

She draped an arm over his broad chest.

He pulled her close and kissed her forehead. "You smell like the saloon."

"Why do you keep talking when you know I only want sleep?" she murmured.

He nuzzled her ear and whispered, "I like the funny way you talk, proper like, and with an accent."

"It's good old Twentieth Century Virginian."

"Huh?"

She had no choice. She kissed Clyde to keep him from speaking. And without further provocation, his fingers stroked the length of her form.

She parted her thighs without any semblance of urgency or desire. His skin was sweaty, his kisses were hungry and moist, and his need was passionate.

She moaned as he mounted her and slid his manhood between her thighs. Slowly he rotated his pelvis as he covered her face with kisses.

"I love you," he whispered.

"I love you, too," she lied and stuck her tongue in his ear.

Their coupling lasted for hours, it seemed. Finally, he climaxed, gave her a peck on the cheek, and rolled off. Soon after, he was snoring.

• • • •

SHE HOVERED IN THE twilight place between sleep and wakefulness. Somewhere far, she heard a strange man's angry demands immediately followed by Clyde's morose pleas.

The man shouted, and then flesh struck flesh. Sara thought of a slap to the face or a fist pounding a jaw. Then, after a moment, she heard Clyde agreeing.

"Yes, suh. Yes, suh."

Alarmed, Sara tried to unseal her eyelids, but exhaustion or intoxication kept them closed. And she drifted off again.

Later, as she struggled to awaken, she grew aware of worse sounds, Midnight's heartbreaking neighing followed by the cracks of a bullwhip. In her dreams, she felt deep lashing bites on her thighs.

She bolted upright with pain burning her skin right like a hot poker. She expected to see a zigzag gash oozing blood when she removed her hand, but her skin was unmarked.

Something was wrong.

Her heart pounded as understanding seeped.

She hurried out of bed, threw on a simple frock, and rushed through the tiny living room to the front door. Clyde called out to her as she scrambled outside, momentarily dazzled by the brilliant sunlight.

The summertime air was stagnant, but she was unaware of her surroundings as she stumbled into the stable. Raw terror fully awakened her even as she prayed that she was having a nightmare.

Her head thundered from a pitiless hangover. Her mouth was as dry as tumbleweeds, yet dread propelled her to his stall, his *empty* stall. She collapsed on all fours and vomited. Clyde was instantly by her side, draping a thick arm around her shoulders.

"Where is he?" She questioned in an emotional and croaky whisper. Then she shouted, "Where the hell is he!" Tears sped down her face and dribbled off her chin.

Clyde, wearing a heavy apron and covered in the muck of his profession, mopped his brow with a thick, blackened glove.

"Please tell me where he is?" she bawled.

Clyde said, "I tried to stop him."

"Who!"

She wanted to curl into a ball and fade away. Or kill someone. Yes, kill.

The singular thought somehow drenched her internal workings with calmness. "Tell me." It was a faint command.

She rose to her feet, brushed the dirt off her nightdress, and claimed Midnight's towel. It was still damp with his sweat. She crushed it to her nose and inhaled his scent.

"I made that thing you wanted. The knucks, right? Ain't that what you called it?" Clyde said without offering any explanation for Midnight's disappearance.

He pressed something Sammy had designed in Sara's hand. Her twin had called them brass knuckles. It was easy to see that he expected some appreciation. She only glared at him.

"I told ya not to be flittin' around, didn't I?" His voice was thick with emotion.

She demanded, "Where is my horse!"

He pulled out a soiled handkerchief from his overalls and wiped his face.

"Stop yakkin' at me, and I will tell ya!" he shouted.

She remained rigid as her eyes dissected him, and then she noticed the burgeoning swell on his left cheek.

"Stop starin' at me like that there!"

Sara looked away and became mute while clenching her teeth from red-hot impatience.

Finally, Clyde heaved in a breath and exclaimed, without meeting her steely gaze, "Mistah Carlson done took him."

The words didn't make sense. "Carlson? Took him?" She sorted through her memories and tried to place the man.

Miller's Town was small, with scarcely a thousand inhabitants, excluding the three hundred or so in Darkie Town. Suddenly the image of Carlson appeared.

The man was a big, red-haired brute. She had often seen him going into Violet's saloon. Other times, she had also seen him accompanying his wife and children to the *white* Baptist church.

She suffered a more recent memory. The doughy man with his gut extending over his belt buckle had once shoved her off the sidewalk. Only an agile leap kept her from landing in horseshit. She also remembered his subsequent robust laughter.

That nasty creature possessed her Midnight?

"I recall him now." It was a whisper.

"Mistah Carlson say he saw you ridin' yo horse last night. He say no nigger was good enuf for a horse like Midnight. He wanted him. I tried to tell him that he weren't my horse to sell. But him didn't care, tho."

Sara couldn't help it. She sobbed freely.

"Don't cry. Tell me what I coulda done different?" Clyde pleaded. "Tell me?"

"Nothing. There was nothing you could've done. A man like that would've killed you," she admitted.

He admonished, "I done tol' you never take that animal out to ride. He a beautiful horse. White folks don't like niggers havin' anythin' better than what they got. I don't tol' you."

Her voice cracked as she agreed. "Yes, you did."

But it wasn't over.

She marched out of the stable, and Clyde followed as she entered the blacksmith shop through a back entrance.

"You cain't hurt a white person. Not in this town, not anywhere. They hang you. Do you hear me?" There was an anxious edge in his tone.

"Don't you understand!" she screamed. "Midnight's the only family I have left. I have to get him back!"

Clyde grabbed her arm and forced her to look into his eyes. "Gotta let it go. You cain't git him back, and you cain't survive carryin' grudges."

She shook herself free.

" 'Sides, ain't I your family too?" he asked.

"You're too good a person for these evil people. You have to leave this town." She caressed his cheekbone. "You're too good to love me."

Gently, he took her hand and kissed her fingers. "You go leave me, ain'tcha?"

"I wish the Stuuwi had made you a necklace too."

"Huh?"

Sara swallowed regret as she said, "It's past time for me to go. It won't be safe for you to stay. Everyone thinks you're my husband. You have to get out. Do you understand?"

"Why? Whatcha go do?"

Luckily the service bell rang and saved her from answering.

"I gotta go see who that is." He ducked into the shop.

She rolled her eyes backward and sent a message. *Midnight? Show me?*

Suddenly, fresh pain zigzagged along her thigh. New injuries joined the old. Through Midnight's eyes, she kicked and snorted in a too-small stall. The snap of the whip caused her to rear up, but she couldn't evade the near-constant cutting stings. The beatings continued even as she fell, bloodied and exhausted. Still, he repeatedly slashed her with the whip.

Their link faded.

Stifling a scream, Sara chastised herself for his predicament. *Don't worry.* She messaged him. *I'm coming for you.*

"Well, don't you look—"

So engrossed in their shared pain that Sara jumped at the familiar sound of her voice.

"—sweet?" Violet's eyes widened. "Clyde said I would find you back here. How did you do that with your eyes?"

She wore her blonde curls piled high, and golden highlights gleamed on the elaborate coif. A sheen of sweat betrayed her calm exterior. She wore a frilly shawl over a high-collared dress and palmed a matching parasol. Without the whorish makeup, Violet appeared younger.

Wordlessly, Sara stripped naked and searched the small bureau for her tan britches and cotton shirt.

"Not bashful, are you?" Violet said, raising her gloved hand to her chin while appraising Sara's nubile body. "Are you sure you don't want to earn some *real* money?"

Sara slipped on her fringed boots and relished the immediate comfort. The simple act of dressing as herself was restorative.

"You can't go out like that," Violet said.

Sara emptied her medicine bag of dried herbs and slipped in the brass knuckles.

"What are those?"

"Never you mind!" Sara snapped.

Once again, she dug inside the bureau and pulled out John Colby's six-shooters and gunbelts. Then, she crisscrossed his belts around her waist and slipped the guns into the holsters.

"Stop!" Violet placed her hand on Sara's shoulder. "I'm here because I heard about the acquiring of your horse."

"Acquiring? That red-faced fucker stole him!"

Violet hurriedly closed the door between the living quarters and the blacksmith shop. "Someone can overhear you."

Violet indicated Sara should sit by aiming her palm at the bed.

Sara did so with reluctance.

Violet peered out the window and scanned the area. Then she sighed with relief. "I don't think anybody heard you."

Then she whispered, "I know you killed John Colby for what he did to you and to your sister. I respect that, but Tom Carlson is different. He is a drunken lout who loses at gambling and likes to poke my girls. But he's a rancher, not a mountain man. The sheriff looks the other way when ranchers cause trouble."

"Do I look as if I'm going to ask the sheriff for help? Besides, I thought you owned the sheriff and this town." Sara retorted.

"I don't own emotions." Violet turned her bluish-purple eyes on Sara. "You do something to Tom, and the law will hunt you down and kill you."

Sara smiled warmly despite the coldness she felt. "But I won't stay dead."

"We all stay dead. That's just part of life."

Sara signaled the discussion was over by grabbing her old cowboy hat from a bureau drawer, pulling it into shape, and fitting it atop her head.

Violet's features hardened. "I know you think you're tough because you got away with killing John Colby. Hell, there was a time or two when I could've killed him. But if you're going after Tom, you must think this through. At least wait until nightfall?"

Sara thought her suggestion was a good idea. Then there was Clyde. The extra hours would give her time to convince him to leave.

"Yes, nightfall would be better. Where can I find Carlson?" Her voice was emotionless.

Violet's shoulders sagged. "All right, s'pose I can't stop you from getting killed. Carlson owns a ranch south of here. Follow the dirt road and take the left branch. Do you know your left from your right?"

Sara nodded without comment.

"Go further along. You can't miss that varmint's spread. It's the only one that way. He's a cattleman with some hands working for him, but they hate the guy. He's stingy and mean. He's got a wife and a couple of kids, a boy and a girl. The wife is good friends with the minister. The boy is mean, a spitting image of his pa."

Sara raised an eyebrow. "And the girl?"

"Beaten down just like her ma."

Sara snapped, "Just like my horse, you mean."

Violet's eyes glazed over with tears. She cupped Sara's face in her soft hands and kissed her lips.

"I don't want you to die," she said. "You're refreshing. You make this dreary town interesting."

Sara said, "If I die, I won't stay dead. Midnight and I will be back. Just do me a favor and watch over Clyde. Get him out of here."

"Well," she said, "I'll drop by later and try to convince him."

Sara's scowl returned as she peered out the window and gazed at the bustling street.

"Be careful," Violet said, kissing Sara's cheek before departing.

Sara watched her leave. Violet's long skirt swirled up clouds of dust as she sashayed to the saloon. Before she entered her establishment, she turned only once to wiggle her fingers in a coy goodbye wave.

A corner of Sara's lips lifted into a smile, which immediately disappeared when she thought of Midnight's dire predicament.

As Sara rolled her belongings inside the saddlebag, Clyde entered the bedroom, his hulking form filling in the door frame.

"I done hear you talkin' to Miss Violet. Whatcha gon do when you gits to his place?"

"Get my horse and ride out."

"Jist like that?" He was somber.

Her eyes were on the horizon. "Nope. I'm going to kill Carlson first." The smile made her lovely face even more beautiful.

13. SUMBITCH

SARA

• • • •

SHE WAS THE LONE PEDESTRIAN on the flat but rocky trail. The sun was setting, and without its heat, the temperature dropped. Sara didn't feel the cold.

Rusty fingers of orange and gold scraped the horizon. Yet, the stars flickering in the encroaching blackness, more than the broken trail, assured she was on the right path.

The expanse offered no cover for natives, banditos, or other riffraff. But at least the solitude was better than the alternative of suffering in the town.

She followed Violet's advice when she reached the fork and took the left path. By the moonlight, she stooped and examined a set of hoofprints. She knew the heavy u-shape of his Midnight's shoes. This discovery belonged to another horse, and the deeper indentation meant he had a heavy rider. The prints weren't fresh, and the shoe direction told her horse and rider had headed for town.

Maybe Tom Carlson had gone out for his gambling and whoring? Maybe he had left Midnight at the ranch?

Maybe.

She quickened her pace. The knife in her right boot and the guns hanging low on her hips added to her hopefulness and feelings of invincibility. Anticipation fluttered in her chest when she finally saw the ramshackle collection of single-story structures.

Since the landscape didn't offer a tree or bush, there was no point in hiding. Meanwhile, the brisk wind chilled the sweat on her skin.

She rolled her eyes backward and mentally called out to him. *Midnight, I'm here.*

There was only blackness. She sensed and saw nothing from him. Naturally, he could die. But he was as protected from death's grip, same as she. He would come back to life. Couldn't he?

The preacher in Darkie Town had said coming back to life after death was a resurrection. Still, she never wanted Midnight to die, *ever.* And she had never tested the magic woven into his mane.

Surprised that her approach had been unobserved, she relished her good luck as she crept alongside the larger of the two buildings. Then she heard snarling and barking dogs and fled to the main structure.

Candlelight ebbed from the windows, and she overheard snatches of the conversation between a woman, a boy, and a girl.

A pair of mongrels emerged from the shadows and snarled at her feet.

Too late, she also heard the click of a rifle hammer. Cold iron pressed behind her ear and forced her to stare straight ahead. Then, suddenly, she caught a whiff of dirt, sweat, and cow shit.

"Git back!" A gruff voice demanded. The dogs whined and retreated, then fled into the darkness.

In a quick, one-two action, the barrel moved from behind her ear to the center of her back.

Sara raised her hands and was prodded toward a smaller building.

Suddenly, the big house's door opened, and a woman, hidden in the shadows, appeared on the porch. A voice, soaked with concern, asked, "What's going on out there? Henry? Earl? Is that you, Tom?"

"It's just me, Miss Winnie, Henry. Everything fine. Dogs found a rabbit. That's all."

"Oh, okay. I hope you have a good night."

"Thank you, Missus. You too."

She went back inside. A little girl's laughter lingered in the night. Briefly, Sara thought of Little Ruthie.

She pondered on that old wound for a second before the barrel poked her back. She continued to the cabin with hands still raised. A leg kicked out from behind, forcing the door open and unsettling the scraggly man sitting at a table eating a plate of beans.

He backhanded his mouth as he eyed her with lustful intent. "What ya got there? Looks like Santy Claus done come early this year?"

The voice behind her said, "I recognize this 'un. This here is Miss Violet's friend. I ain't partial to dark meat, but I'm willing to give it a try." Henry's laughter was dry and sinister. Then he shoved her inside the cabin, a one-room shack.

She calculated the gun pressed against her spine was the immediate threat. Could she swing aside and grab the gun at the same time? A cunning smile lifted the corner of her lips. Yes, she could do it.

"Whatcha smiling at—" Earl didn't get the chance to finish his sentence.

She twisted away from the rifle. A shot went off. She grabbed the barrel with one hand and drove her fingers into Henry's eyes with the other.

He howled and clapped a hand over his face and jigged.

She aimed at the beans eater and fired.

Earl jerked as a section of his face peeled from his head and splattered the wall. He fell forward, with the remnants of his skull landing on his plate

Henry flailed about with eyes closed. "Earl! Did you get her?"

"No," Sara said as she unsheathed her knife. "He didn't get me."

She drove the blade into his chest and twisted. Just then, a woman appeared in the doorway. She wore a horrified expression on her face. Then she clamped both hands over her mouth as she slowly backed out of the cabin.

"Don't run," Sara warned as she leveled the rifle at her. "I don't want to hurt you or your children."

The woman froze.

At that moment, she felt Midnight. Sara suspected the gun blasts had probably awakened him. "Here. I am here." She said out loud.

"What? I don't understand what you want me to do. What do you mean?" The woman said in a trembling voice.

"I wasn't talking to you," Sara snapped.

The woman may have been lovely once, but harsh living in the Plains and perhaps an even harsher marriage had washed any youthful exuberance from her features. She was pale, almost gray, and her face bore many creases like careworn fabric.

The woman begged. "Please, take what you want and go away."

Sara stared into her brown eyes and knew. She recognized the fretful behavior of someone who lived a bullied life.

"My husband will be home soon."

"That's what I'm waiting for," Sara said.

She used the gun barrel the same way the dead man had used it on her and herded the frightened woman across the yard and into her home.

The interior of the house was nicely furnished. A fire crackled in the hearth. The aroma of cooked meat and something sweet, perhaps pie, lingered in the air. At that moment, Sara realized she hadn't eaten all day.

The two children anxiously observed their entrance. The girl, about seven, had enormous eyes on a small face. Sara thought about how she appeared less afraid than her mother. And she thought the girl's bravery was adorable.

The boy, a towhead of around twelve, strode up to her, his young chest inflated. He placed both hands on his hips and spat at her feet. "My father is going to kill you," he assured her.

Sara lowered the rifle and slapped his face. He reeled backward, cupped his cheek, and ran to his mother.

The woman motioned for her daughter and clutched both children by her side.

Then, using the rifle, Sara ushered them into the kitchen, where she pulled out a chair and sat.

"May I have something to eat, please?"

The woman nodded as if grateful for something to do. The little girl, with her mother's dark brown hair, studied Sara carefully.

"My name is Abby. What's your name?"

The mother was slicing meat. Sara watched as she held the knife and considered her options. The boy was nearby, whispering to his mother.

Sara could only guess their discussion. Her attention returned to the little girl. "Abby, that's a pretty name. My name is Raven."

"Like the bird?"

Sara smiled. "Yes, like the blackbird."

The woman placed a plate of thick meat and corn stew on the table. Sara was salivating. "That looks good. What's your name?"

"Martha."

She handed Sara a knife and fork.

The boy snapped. "You silly bitch! I told you to stab her with it."

Sara lunged for the boy and grabbed his throat. "Don't you talk to your mother like that! You don't know how lucky you are to have a mother!"

Martha cried, "Please don't hurt Johnnie! He means no harm!"

"All right, I won't. Get me some rope."

Martha disappeared, but she returned to the room with a length of rope.

Johnnie screamed, "Dammit! Why didn't you run for help? Dad's right! You're a stupid woman!"

When Martha cowered from her son, Sara struck the boy again. This time harder. A red welt marred his belligerent face. She got up, grabbed his collar, and slammed him onto the nearest chair. Then, as she carefully eyed mother and daughter, she tied him to the chair without any measure of delicacy. Then using the knife, she sliced off a piece of Martha's dress and used it to gag her son.

Abby giggled behind her tiny hands.

"There. That's better." After appreciating her handiwork, Sara returned to her seat and began gobbling her food. Then, after a few bites, she winked at Abby and asked. "Where were we?"

"I like you, Raven. You look like a gunslinger. Are you a gunslinger?" The child watched her with awe.

Sara thought as she shoved corn into her mouth. "I'm not a gunslinger," she said as she simultaneously glanced down at the weapon on her hip while scooping up another spoonful of food.

"Where you from?"

"I'll tell you the truth," she said and softened her life's story as best she could. But the watered-down retelling moistened both their eyes and almost made her forget her real mission. Almost.

Martha joined them at the table, only rising occasionally to pour fresh water into Sara's cup while the two talked. When the hour grew late, and after dribbling her tale with some mysticism to delight the young girl, Abby's eyes sealed, and her head started bobbing. Sara allowed Martha to put her to bed.

Another hour slowly passed. Martha sat in a rocking chair and darned a shirt. Occasionally she lapsed into humming a tune.

Sara was bewildered by the woman's calmness. When Martha tilted her head, Sara saw purple bruises on her neck. She remembered Violet's obvious disdain when describing Tom Carlson as a brute and a whorish gambler.

Sara settled in a chair that strategically faced the door and gave her an open view of the room.

Hours after the hot meal, she fought the urge to sleep. Staying alert was difficult. She held the cup of water precariously on her lap. She hoped draining the last swig of liquid would keep her awake.

By now, Martha had slumped in the chair. Her eyes were closed, and her mouth hung open. The sewing lay in the center of her lap.

Johnnie was awake. Although he'd ceased squirming against his ropes, he stared at Sara with unblinking hatred. The material gagging his mouth was sopping from saliva.

She grinned.

Suddenly, Midnight whinnied, and he sounded agitated.

She heard the dogs barking and the loud clopping of a horse. Moments later, and on the opposite side of the front door, a man's rough voice slurred, off-key, a ribald ditty.

Johnnie gave a muffled scream.

The song choked off in the mid-chorus.

Sara drew the six-shooter and leaped behind the door. She expected to hear his heavy-booted steps on the porch. Instead, she listened to his clumsy dash to the ranch hands' quarters.

Her heart thumped wildly, and she grabbed the door handle.

Martha rested her hand on Sara's.

In a fluid motion, she turned and pointed. But only sheer willpower prevented her from taking the shot.

"Make sure you do the job right. I want that sumbitch dead," Martha whispered through clenched teeth, her weathered face contorted with hatred.

Sara looked over her shoulder at the boy squirming violently for his freedom. "I certainly will. Blow out the candles."

Martha quickly blew out the lanterns and hovered close to her son.

Sara threw open the door.

The moonlight shone on an unbridled mottled grey and white horse. Yet, despite the luminescence washing over the landscape, Sara blended with the shadows elongating from the house.

The air was cold, and the atmosphere was still. Sara strained to hear any sound in the vacuum of silence. She thought of merging with Midnight to share his sight, but she couldn't take the chance of dividing her concentration.

Her grip tightened on the gun. Again, she wondered about her supposed immortality. Maybe she had been lucky.

A man's silhouette crept outside the ranch hands' cabin. Only a slight dip in his step indicated his intoxication. He ran to the other side of the structure and disappeared. Sara hunched as she bolted to the cabin.

There was a long, low whistle.

She heard the dogs before she saw them. As soon as they scampered from black obscurity, she fired three shots in rapid succession. The dogs all collapsed—two whimpered.

Tom emerged from an adjacent bank of shadows as silently as the wind. Sara was startled by his nearness. A coarse brute who loomed over her and grinned as if she were prey. His crooked grin turned callous as he punched her face and dislocated her jaw.

Before she could fully register her pain, he drove his fist into her abdomen, forcing her to drop her gun. She turned, but not fast enough, and the brute kicked her right leg. First, she heard and then felt the bone break.

Hurting in different parts of her body, Sara could only sink in a cloud of dust. She tasted blood in her mouth while some streamed down her chin. In the distance, Midnight whinnied.

"What's the matter, little girl?" Tom snickered, "Did you come here for your horse? Do I get to break you first? Martha needs a maid. You know you did me a favor, killing those fools. At least I don't have to pay 'em."

Then, chuckling, he added, "I'll say the injuns came to raid."

His glee turned mean as he raised his foot over her face. The reek of hooch and sour perfume wafted downward and re-ignited a fiery hatred. At the last second, Sara rolled away from his stomp.

Still, he lunged and gripped her neck and squeezed.

She gasped and wheezed as he strangled her, digging his fingernails into her skin.

Then, in a speedy blur, she reached inside her boot and yanked the knife out of its sheath. Holding her mother's old knife was akin to tapping an ancient power. She had just enough energy for a quick yet penetrating thrust.

Shock replaced his smug expression, and he convulsed as a soft whelping noise loosened from his throat.

She withdrew the blade and gored his chest, adding a stiff-wristed twist with a superior grunt. She sidestepped him as he slumped on the ground with the stiffness of a downed tree. Broken, Sara cleaned the knife by swiping it on her trousers as she glared at his corpse.

She tenderly touched her jaw. Slivers of pain ricocheted

Midnight neighed.

She limped toward him, holding her stomach, and drew in a lungful of the cold air as she ambled her way to the stalls. She had taken only a few steps when the pain eased.

Soon the ache in her stomach vanished, and her gait became steadier and more self-assured, unencumbered by pain. By the time she reunited with her beloved Midnight, she had fully recovered.

Midnight tossed his dark-maned head at her arrival and reared onto his hind legs.

Tears leaked down her face as she kissed and rubbed his nose. Then she led him outside and checked his coat. His hide was unblemished.

"You too? Maybe we are immortal."

Her heart joyously skipped as she wrapped her arms around his long, sleek neck and hugged him tightly. She kissed him repeatedly.

"It's time to go," she said after a time.

She retrieved her saddlebag from the ranchhand's quarters, scowled at the dead bodies, and hurried back to the stall. She spotted a more superior saddle hanging on a nearby gate. She plucked it, sniffed the fresh leather, and smiled at her horse. "I think I will take this one."

She emptied the new saddlebag and stuffed it with her belongings before leading Midnight out of the stable. True peace only came when she mounted her stallion. She was rejuvenated by the subtle motion of his rhythmic breathing between her thighs. She tightened her grip on the reins and gave him a gentle nudge as the pair headed in the opposite direction of Miller's Town.

14. SONOVABITCH

****SAMMY*****

• • • •

AN ORDERLY ACCOMPANIED her to the new psychiatrist's office. He hadn't been there for two days before rumors circulated among staff and eavesdropping patients.

Dr. Amari was a foreigner who spoke with an enthralling and thick accent. Gossip also hinted that he was a strict disciplinarian who demanded perfection and compliance.

Oh, and by the way, he was also gorgeous.

Sammy caught her breath when she first saw him because he was hunky eye candy.

He looked to be in his mid-thirties, at most. Since he had chestnut-colored, wavy hair, and copper skin, she wondered if he was Egyptian. And she found his brown eyes under thick black brows riveting.

He rose from his seat and shook her hand warmly. "Hi there, Miss Montgomery. I will be with you in just a minute."

"Sure."

She watched as he reclaimed his seat and silently heaved at the deep tenor of his sultry voice.

This doctor was much younger than old Dr. Pender and more handsome than alien-looking Dr. Gibson.

His predecessor, Dr. Pender, had been an unyielding mouse who pushed meds instead of listening. She had never trusted the nasal-voiced man who spied her through bifocals, which he furiously rubbed with a white handkerchief whenever she mentioned Sara's name.

While Dr.Gibson, the Shock'em King, had been just plain weird.

Dr. Pender retired with almost no fanfare, although she wished she could have sent him to his field of dreams with a foot up his ass.

Now Dr. Amari sat behind the familiar massive desk, reading papers in a file.

Sammy mused, *Yep, thick enough to be my file.*

She hoped to convince him she was sane. After all, her best friend *was* real, although they *only* met in a place called Nysa, which resembled how heaven ought to look.

Gawd! Her reality seemed loony toons as she mentally pieced her talking points together. A part of her realized trying to convince any doctor that Sara existed was absurd.

She plopped onto the soft leather chair and waited for his attention. She gnawed her fingernails while pumping her right leg in nervous hope. Her focus shifted to the bookshelf. She angled her head as she read the spines, *Trauma, Dissociative Identity Disorder, Abnormal Children and Aberrant Adolescence, Neurotic Symptoms*. Scanning those few titles was heartbreaking, so she stopped.

Her interest drifted beyond the plexiglass window. Outside, the sun shone brightly, and baby sprouts budded on a nearby tree.

Sammy was unaware of the day or date and found her lack of knowing something so basic depressing. Renewed hopelessness sagged her shoulders. Overall, she was merely tired of therapies and pills. At least, with Dr. Gibson reassigned, she was spared the hazy rituals of electric shock treatments.

Then she thought of how easily Zeus kept her saner than those godawful pills. And she thanked God for her ability to explore the world from his eyes.

It didn't matter if his view came from a waist-high position because, if he hadn't shared his explorations through his wolfish eyes, Sammy would've gone apeshit in the wacky house, for real. Besides the diminished vantage point, she recognized, through their pairing, how life's colors appeared less vibrant to him. But that was okay, too. The real problem was his insufferable and constant obsession with chasing squirrels, which revved up her angst.

Finally, Dr. Amari looked up from his papers and dismissed the orderly with a slight wave.

"Pleased to meet you, Samantha. Or do you prefer Sammy? Sorry for the delay. My Meet and Greets have been running a little long."

The deep tenor of his voice made her smile.

"Sure, I don't stand on formality here, doc. May I call you...?"

"...Dr. Amari," he finished.

"Then I insist you can call me Miss Montgomery."

His smile was easy. "The notes say you prefer Sammy. Listen, I think we're starting on the wrong foot, and I don't want that. I want to help you get better."

Sammy draped a leg over the chair arm. Ah, yes, she knew *this* speech. "Sure, you do."

He jotted on a pad.

Here we go, she thought. A few lousy sentences and Dr. Amari already concurred with the rubbish he had just read.

His gaze pierced hers. *Damn, he's good-looking,* she mused.

She said, "Let me guess. My initial diagnosis of post-traumatic stress disorder was upgraded— I think that's the right word—to a dissociative identity disorder. Or, in layman's terms, multiple personality disorder, then schizotypal personality disorder. And no, I don't have bodily illusions or think magic is real."

After her rant, she sighed with a huff. "I mean, gunning down schoolmates, rape, and then giving birth to my rapist's child might make anyone a little cray-cray? But I'm fine now."

He rocked back in his chair and tilted his head. "Your record says you're brilliant. I know I love the twist on your names."

She frowned. "What twist?"

He tapped an expensive-looking silver pen on his lips. "Sammy and Sara."

"Not following, Doc."

He shrugged. "Okay, I'll play by explaining. In Buddhism, Samsara is about birth, death, and rebirth. In your file, you state that Sara is from a different time. The late 1800s? You say she looks like you. You've even called her your twin, and that you can only meet in a place called Nysa. Is it Nysa or Nirvana? I can't remember." He began flicking pages.

"What? Huh?"

"Do you believe *you* were Sara in a previous life?"

Sammy started giggling. When she calmed, she said, between laughs. "Sara and I exist simultaneously. We always have, she lives in her time stream, and I live in mine."

He leaned forward, "Okay, I'll bite. Time streams?"

"Maybe we aren't in a universe, but we exist in a multiverse, and somehow Sara and I have connected. We have nothing to do with Buddhism or Nirvana. Our names are just a coincidence."

A knock on the door interrupted their conversation.

The orderly leaned in. "Your next appointment is ready, and Sammy has a group meeting."

"Okay, Hal," he said.

"That's it?" Sammy asked, failing to shield her anger.

Dr. Amari stood and extended his hand. "I would like to continue the daily schedule you had with Dr. Pender. Is that okay?"

She gave him a limp handshake. "Do I have a choice?"

With that, her session ended.

She followed Hal to a large room where everyone else was already seated in a circle.

The therapist was Dr. Linden, a sullen, middle-aged woman who sometimes exhibited agitated movements like a chicken, hence her nickname, Chicken Wing.

The only available seat was beside Camila, the self-proclaimed psychic.

Sammy plopped in the chair with tart frustration lingering on her tongue.

Camila whispered, "Is he as cute as they say?"

"Yes," tumbled from her lips.

"What's wrong with you?"

Sammy shook her head. "Nothing."

But there was something wrong. Despite the gobbledygook she had sprouted to Dr. Amari, she had never really tried to figure out Sara's existence. Sara was, and together they were, simple enough to understand. Right?

Chicken Wing cleared her throat. "Ladies, would you like to share?"

Camila piped up. "Well, I asked Sammy if Dr. Amari is a hottie! And she said yes!"

Karen, a thick girl with china-doll features and long ropy braids, said, "You got that right!"

The mutterings increased while the teenage boys snorted their disapproval.

"All right, settle down." Chicken Wing directed her question to Sammy. "How are you today? You look a little down. Is there anything you want to talk about?"

She didn't want to share her silly twinges of how a different religion might explain Sara's presence. But their names, Sammy and Sara, well, that was too much of a coincidence.

After the group session, she sank onto one of the overly soft couches in the lounge and stared at the television screen anchored near the ceiling.

Hours later, Camila, snacking on chips, plunked beside her uninvited, then she opened the bag wider and offered.

"Nah." Sammy had no appetite.

"You're right. The new doc is dreamy," Camila said. "He's slick too, don't you think? I mean, I don't have a whatchamacallit? Antisocial personality?"

"Don't suck that stuff up."

Camila asked, "How can I be antisocial? I like people. I like you. Just 'cuz I knifed my stepdad for slipping his fingers in me, I'm here. It was self-defense. Bastard's lucky he lived."

Camila's incessant chattering gave her a headache. It was almost time for chow. Maybe she could escape by joining a group for dinner.

"She's real, you know." Camila plucked a broken potato chip from the bag and ate it with relish.

"Stop it." It came out as a whisper.

Camila blew into the empty bag and popped it by slamming her palm against the impromptu balloon. The loud bang caused a series of nervous commotions in the room. Screams spiked with laughter, more hair pulled from scalps, and someone overturned a game table.

Hal confiscated the empty bag. "Very funny," he snapped.

Camila chuckled, "I thought so." She scraped the chip remnants from her gums and sucked on her index finger. While staring at the television, she said, "Last night, I dreamt Sara killed a man. He was a nasty motherfucker too."

"Please stop with your bullshit. You're making my head hurt." Sammy could feel her face grow warm.

Camila was undeterred. "Doctors don't know shit. Dr. A. may be cute, but let's face it, he's a sonovabitch just like the others."

"Maybe," Sammy said. "He gave me plenty to think about."

"Yeah, yeah. Well, I can only tell you what I saw. When I'm near you, I see all kinds of crap. You're like a battery or whatever. I wish you were around me before that fucker fingered my va-jay-jay. I coulda used a warning then."

"Me too," she said sincerely.

Camila hugged her and kissed her temple. "You really are a good person. Trust me when I say you're different. Cuz you are. Sara is real. She can't die, you know that, right? She and that horse of hers."

Midnight?

Sammy perked up. She'd never told anyone about Midnight. "Sara's got this mojo thing hanging around her neck. She thinks the—what does she call that thing—Stew-something gave it to her. But it wasn't the Stew-thing or her Mom. Sara's just plain powerful, but she's too blind to see it."

A faraway look bloomed on Camilla's face. "She's got a gift for you too. I hope she hurries up, cuz we need to later this damn place, for real."

Sammy glared at her friend. There it was, a belief in magic. She said, "At least Sara knew her mom loved her. Mine is MIA. I haven't seen her since I gave birth to—" She blinked back tears.

The dinner bell sounded.

Sammy added, "Thanks for trying to make me feel better."

"Sure! I hope you don't mind that I told my brother about you. He wants to meet you. He's cute. Well, I think so anyway."

Camila pulled her from the couch, and they filed out of the room with the others. "I wish I could do the mind meld-thing with Zeus? You're always happier after you do it. You should piggyback on his brain more often."

Sammy opened her mouth in shock. "How do you know about Zeus and me?"

Camila gave her a teasing shove down the hallway. "Girl, I'm psychic." Then she whispered, "Guess what? You're going to come up with a plan to break us out of this hellhole."

15. CLYDE

****SARA****

....

FOR DAYS SARA ROAMED the Plains without purpose or even a destination. Yet, she found a measure of peace living as a nomad. She didn't know much of the world, only having existed in the village with her people before seeking shelter with her sister Butterfly and ending up with Clyde in Miller's Town.

But she did remember her mother's stories about her life as a slave.

Ruthie had suffered and survived mental and physical bondage, degradation, and desperation. She had freed herself by killing the slave owner and his family before fleeing into the hostile unknown. Luckily she had met her father, Black-eyed Wolf, and had found peace with the people.

Sara wasn't sure if she was as strong as her mother. She had hated living in the village and often avoided remembering the massacre that claimed her parents.

The terrain was dry under Midnight's hooves. The aridness worked its way into her eyes, mouth, and the creases in her skin. And yet, the harshness of the land offered something she'd rarely experienced in her young life: serenity. Rabbit meat was plentiful, and Midnight fed on the brush. But, water was scarce, and she filled up her canteen whenever they happened upon a stream.

She avoided interactions with tribes and homesteaders since no people meant no scrutiny.

During a late-night thick with the promise of rain, she coaxed the dying embers of the evening fire. She contemplated tossing in another buffalo chip but decided against it. She didn't want to risk drawing unwanted attention. So she allowed the light to die out. She unfurled her bedroll and curled under a thin blanket with her saddlebag as a makeshift pillow. The six-shooter was within easy reach, the knife was outside its sheath, and the shiny blade glinted from the fading firelight. Even the rabbit bones were buried. A full belly and a face slick from animal fat lured her into a comfortable slumber.

The grisly nightmare began at once and ripped apart her brief tranquility. She awakened with a crying upright jerk. Despite rousing, she couldn't *un-hear* the ghostly cries for help or the twisted black faces coated in blood. Tears squeezed from her eyes. Clyde's name lingered on her lips.

Midnight nuzzled the top of her head as if to comfort her.

She was rarely constricted by morality or conscience, but she wondered if she had been wrong to flee without ensuring his safety.

But Violet had promised.

And Clyde was a stubborn creature.

How would anyone know she had killed those men? *Dammit!* She had left witnesses. She recalled Johnnie's hateful stare. *Dammit!*

She tried to go back to sleep. She tried to convince herself it had only been a dream, a too-real nightmare. But the disjointed fragments resurfaced each time she closed her eyes. She heard angry white voices demanding justice, and then she saw Darkie Town engulfed in flames.

Clyde? Please, God, Nesaru, or Obatala, keep him safe.

She promptly rolled up the bedding, piled her meager belongings into the saddlebag, and tied everything to the saddle, before mounting Midnight.

For days they swiftly rode straight back to Hell. Then, minutes before daybreak, they arrived at Miller's Town. Charred brick and timber remnants stood in the place of the once-prosperous blacksmith shop.

Midnight whinnied and shook his head as he backed away from the ruin. But fear muted Sara. Her revenge had demanded a high price, after all. She also trembled because, in her heart, she knew he hadn't escaped as she'd hoped.

She whispered as her heart hammered against her ribs, "Clyde?" Tears rolled down her cheeks.

Reluctantly, she turned Midnight around and guided him to Darkie Town.

"Whoa!"

It was gone. And like the blacksmith shop, only decimated ruin remained where a fire had licked most homes to near cinders.

Yet, there was devastating evidence everywhere of a ruthless attack. Although Sara didn't see whole bodies, blood, torn limbs, and gore showed the extent of the brutality, chaos, and savagery.

She urged Midnight to travel further down a road once lined with well-kept shacks. She halted him at the blackened skeleton of the poorly stocked general store. She dismounted, still weighed by grief and guilt, and crept inside. The only patrons were scurrying rodents and hungry mongrels.

Frozen with a heavy heart and unblinking eyes, Sara lost time amid the wreckage. The obliteration of her childhood village mentally rearranged over the debris of Darkie Town. The destructive similarities bombarded her with unimaginable torment.

She released a silent scream. It was either that or explode. She clutched hands full of hair and tore them out by the roots. She needed to feel the pain as she backed out of the store, and she hugged herself.

"My fault," she cried. "I know this is all my fault!"

Midnight neighed, bumped her head with his nose, and snapped her back to reality. She wrapped her arms around his thick neck and wept. After an eon, she dried her tears and eased into the saddle.

She didn't know how long she'd stayed in the dead town listening to the ghosts of doomed Negroes pleading for help. The evening sun hung low when she accepted the growing stoniness of her heart. She rode Midnight to the other side of town, where the true horror revealed itself.

The tree was immense, so large the upper limbs appeared to claw the sky. The Darkie Town inhabitants had remained. Men, women, and children swayed on the branches like ornaments. She was accustomed to the raw stench of death, but this smell was suffocating as she neared the tree.

Was this really because of me?

She prayed and hoped as she searched the masses of strung-up dead bodies for Clyde. When she found him, a low moan rumbled from her throat and passed her lips as a profound and everlasting bawl. She tumbled off Midnight, rose to her knees, and crawled under the swaying remains of his naked body.

His hands were bound behind his back. His eyes had been gouged out, and jagged lacerations exposed meat and bone around the eye sockets. His genitals were missing. The burn marks on his naked buttocks were evidence of his exquisite torture.

Flashes of their brief union flitted over her corneas. His kindness, gentle demeanor, and loving nature mutilated her psyche as the hardness burrowing in her heart expanded. She wiped her teary face and once again mounted her horse. Then she rode back to Darkie Town, where she witnessed two men entering a still standing shanty. They didn't notice her as they hurried in and out, toting items and loading them onto a cart.

Sara, still on horseback, drew her gun and at once welcomed the heaviness of the grip in her palm. She aimed and fired two rapid shots. The men jerked, dropping their loot, before sinking to the ground.

She made a clicking sound with her tongue, and Midnight clip-clopped forward. When they were above the looters' bodies, she leaned over, hawked, and spat on both. She dismounted, unhitched their horses, and led them to a watering trough. Then, after the horses appeared to have drunk their fill, she tied them to the back of a scrap of a burnt-out building, keeping them out of sight from the main road. Then she foraged some hay and fed them.

She filled her canteen from a pump and drank long to wash out the condensed wad of dust that had accumulated in the back of her throat.

In the remains of the general store, she rooted around, kicking aside rubble, and freed a few treasures: a tin cup, plate, and a coffee pot. She was also lucky enough to discover a box of flint and tinder. Now it would be easier to make a fire.

It was apparent to her that food had been pilfered. Still, she hunted through discards and found some salt pork, hardtack, and coffee.

Lingering in Darkie Town until after nightfall, she unbridled the marauders' horses and slapped their backsides, sending them to roam about freely.

Finally, in the wee hours of the early morning, Sara decided she was ready. First, she rode to the Carlson ranch and peered through a window where she spied Martha serenely stitching a garment as she rocked in her chair. Nearby, little Abby played with a ragdoll while her brother whittled.

It was Johnnie who first looked up. Briefly, their eyes met, and then the boy darted for the gun belt hanging on a wall hook.

Sara shot the lock on the door and kicked it in. Martha screamed at the sound while Abby dashed out of the room. Sara's face was as rigid as timber. She narrowed her eyes as she pointed her gun at Johnnie. He froze and raised his hands.

Sara had to know the truth, so as she eyed Martha, she asked, "Why did they burn Darkie Town?"

"I—I—I don't know," Martha stammered, yet her downcast eyes indicated otherwise.

Sara pulled back the hammer. The click resonated in the silence.

"What did you say happened to your husband?" Sara asked.

"I told them Indians attacked us," Martha said, tearing up as she did so. "Please, don't hurt my boy."

"I would be doing the world a favor if I put a bullet right between his eyes. We both know it," Sara snarled.

Johnnie scowled as if daring her to shoot. "You ain't nothing but a nigger half-breed. There's a bounty on your head for killing my Pa, and I'm aiming to collect it!"

Sara sneered, "You told them, didn't you!"

"Ma lied, made up some story, but I told them Clyde's whore killed my Pa and his boys. They let me ride with them. You should've heard Clyde crying like a baby. He shat his pants too. That's why I set fire to his black ass!"

Sara barely contained her rage. She walked over and slapped his belligerent face. Her palm stung from the forceful whack. She wanted to kill him but didn't. Perhaps it was the way Martha's silently pleaded for his life. But, despite her misgivings, Sara restrained her anger.

Instead, she snatched the gun off the wall and left. While on horseback and bolting to Miller's Town, she heard gun blasts. Some bullets found purchase in the ground near Midnight's hooves. Meanwhile, Little Johnnie's maniacal laughter floated in the wind.

Sara continued undaunted. She decided not to take the direct route into Miller's Town. Instead, she dismounted and led Midnight along the littered and unkempt backside of town where only a few idling drunks lingered.

By now, the hour was late, and in all likelihood, the *respectable* people were in bed for the night. However, the sounds of the piano playing mingling with a lively ruckus came from the saloon. But, given what she'd seen, she found their carousing obscene.

She tugged Midnight's reins, forced his head down, and whispered in his ear, "Tonight, I'm going to need you to be lightning fast."

A nod was his response.

She retrieved the tinderbox from his saddle. Then she kissed his face, slapped his backside, and watched as his galloping form merged with the shadows.

She also slipped into the darkness and crept to the place where she assumed the riot had most likely begun, at Clyde's blacksmith's shop.

She collected some wood bits, knelt among the wreckage, and opened the tinderbox. Her memories of Clyde and what had become of him forced her tears and solidified her determination.

She struck the flint with her blade to produce sparks and then nurtured a fiery blaze. She tucked the box in the small medicine bag tied around her waist and returned her attention to the fire. She continued feeding the flames. Eventually, she freed a small section of partially burnt lumber, dipped it into the fire, and carried the torch outside, which she used to set fire to the nearest *respectable* home. She only stayed long enough to see the fire blossom, and then she repeated the process on each house and establishment on one side of the main thoroughfare.

"Sorry, Violet," she murmured.

She intended to scorch the entire town, but screams and outright panic erupted before she could reach the other side.

Flames brightened the clear night like a false daylight while billowing smoke drifted heavenward. At once, it seemed, coughing residents spilled from their burning homes. The ones on fire danced or rolled on the ground in desperation. Others rushed from their houses to see about the commotion. Shrieks of alarm, surprise, and anguish rang with the same vigor as the bombastic peals from the church bell.

To Sara, the chaos was exquisite but certainly wasn't enough. She ran behind the saloon, climbed the back steps, and mounted the roof with the agility of a spider.

From her perch, she visually feasted on the fear and confusion and received their soulful screams as sweet music.

Now, she watched men fruitlessly fill buckets from troughs and wells to throw on the inferno. Their actions only seemed to feed the blazes. She admired her handiwork in the quivering phony daylight, fascinated as the flames moved like a greedy entity. It leaped from building to building, fueled by a dry wind.

Some of the townfolk wandered about as if shocked, while others panicked and ran aimlessly while a few men in bed clothing tried to douse the fire.

The visible and rampant chaos was the moment Sara had awaited. She lowered onto her knees and aimed.

Her first shot took down the sheriff as he prepared to toss a bucket of water on a burning building. The bullet passed through his neck, and his blood sprayed the deputy by his side. Sara spared the next lawman any shock by taking out his right eye. The deputy was dead before he sank to the ground.

She absorbed her early rushes of exhilaration as she picked off four more citizens, reloaded her favorite gun, and quickly claimed the lives of another six.

High-pitched screams punctuated the night as the fleeing townies scattered from her attack.

A boyish and familiar voice shouted. "Look! She's up there!"

Riding on horseback, Little Johnnie pointed out her roost as he descended his steed and fired. His bullet nicked her hat. She wasn't angry. With a sly smile, she silently apologized to Martha and returned fire. The bullet drilled precisely where she had wanted to put it hours earlier.

By now, a shower of bullets chased her from the perch. Luckily for her, scampering down the building was quicker than the climb.

Midnight arrived without summoning to the backside of the saloon.

Sara mounted in a two-legged leap, but not before taking a nasty hit to the shoulder. She felt a blinding pressure and saw blood oozing down her pant leg. Her injury was of no consequence because they had to escape.

Midnight charged through the chaos by navigating the terrain with ease. The pair rode as if the steed and rider were a single demonic entity.

She, breathing hard while he, snorting, blended into the safety of the surrounding darkness.

But they weren't alone.

An angry swarm had quickly gathered. The posse charged after Sara with a savage purpose. Shots were fired but missed their mark because of the wide gap between hunters and prey.

She should've been scared. She should've entertained thoughts of "what if." What if she was captured and had her eyes plucked out before being hung from a tree?

But she didn't.

There were no "what ifs" in her mind. She didn't feel fear or remorse. Instead, she only relished the euphoric high of raw exhilaration.

The landscape was a blur until Midnight neighed and then stumbled. They hit the ground hard. Sara ignored her bruises and scrapes. Immediately, she worried he had been shot and checked on his well-being.

"Are you okay?" she asked, favoring her arm as she swept a hand over his torso.

A cursory examination indicated no injuries, and in reality, her arm was also feeling better. But they were almost out of time. The posse was gaining distance.

"Ready?"

Midnight nodded.

Yet, when she climbed atop him, her hand was slick with blood. Before she could react, he took off. Despite their brief stop and his apparent wound, he continued outpacing the inferior animals trailing him. The distance between her and the posse increased until their rancor died, and they were nothing more than specks. And then nothing more.

16. WANTED

*****SARA*****

• • • •

I'M OFFICIALLY AN OUTLAW, she thought, musing on her circumstances the following day as she and Midnight moseyed into a town where the poorly scrawled "Welcome" sign stated the place was called Harmony.

Exhausted and hungry, she strode the dusty streets with Midnight in tow as she sought a place to bed down.

The homes in Harmony were superior to the slapdash houses in Miller's Town. These houses had individual porches and glass windows with shutters. Some residences had plots of land with small gardens of blooming flowers or vegetables.

The citizens didn't regard her with the near-constant veneer of sneering contempt—if they looked at her at all. And no one seemed alarmed that she was dirty or wore dried blood on her clothing. But nobody offered her any assistance.

Soon, she arrived at the part of Harmony where it appeared the Negroes congregated. She hoped the area was Harmony's version of Darkie Town.

She stopped a young fair-skinned black woman with long black hair and asked, "Is there a place where I can sleep and get some food for me and my horse?"

The woman's light brown eyes swept over Sara's ragged appearance. "There's a rooming house just yonder." She pointed to a nearby two-story structure. "Don't think you can afford it. You might have to sleep outside. It looks like you're used to that."

Sara had no money. She'd learned from living with Clyde that currency meant everything in the whites' world.

"You're right. Thank you," Sara replied.

Weariness settled in her bones. They had been riding off and on for hours, had eluded a posse, and still, they had many miles to go before Sara could possibly feel safe.

She turned to leave when the young woman opened a petite purse and pressed some coins in her hand.

Sara was so overwhelmed by the kindness that she blinked back tears of gratitude. Killing was easy. Accepting kindness was hard.

"Thank you," she said once again.

The young woman merely nodded and walked away.

Sara led Midnight to the rooming house and hitched him to the post. She waited as he drank from the trough and examined his coat. She spotted blood but no wound, although she had discovered the hole earlier.

The stinging in her shoulder had long since faded. She tapped the spot. Nothing. No blood, no wound, or blemish.

She unhitched her saddlebag and entered the establishment. It took seconds for her eyes to adjust to the subdued lighting. She noticed how the interior was cool and fragrant with freshly baked bread. Her stomach growled, a gnawing response.

Behind a desk stood a rotund man with a bald pate and a superior attitude. He frowned just a bit at her approach. He focused on her dirty clothing before resting on the holstered six-shooters.

"May I help you?" His voice dripped with disdain. Then he scrunched his nose and took a backward step when she leaned on the registration desk.

"Yes, I need a room and a bath."

"How long will you be staying?" He smirked as if convinced she couldn't afford his rates.

Sara placed two bits on the counter. "Not long. A couple of days." She pushed another bit across the desk. "Need some food."

His demeanor instantly changed. With a toothy smile, he said, "Certainly. I'll have my daughter prepare your bath."

He reached into the desk drawer and slapped a key on the counter. "We serve lunches at noon and dinners at six. If you miss those times, then you don't eat here."

"What time is it now?"

He said sourly, "Noon."

"Have it brought to my room." Sara picked up the key and looked for the number. "There isn't a number on here."

"You can read?"

"Yep. Why not? Because I look like a savage? You're an idiot." It was her turn to smirk.

He cleared his throat at her admonishment. "It's the second floor and down the hall. You can't miss it. The door is open."

She would have to climb the stairs. Damn, she was so tired. She took a deep sigh and began the mount.

Midway up the stairs, she hollered, "Oh, and bring me a bottle of whiskey." Then she gritted her teeth as she slowly continued. "The good stuff!" she added.

The red carpeting on the stairs was worn and stained, but the steps and handrails were sturdy, which Sara used for support as she continued her stiff-legged climb.

The room was tiny, with one small window overlooking the street below. From her vantage point, she only saw Midnight's tail as he occasionally swished at flies.

The iron bed took up most of the space. Other furnishings included a wooden chair, a small wall lamp, and wall hooks.

Sara sat on the lumpy bed, removed her boots, and placed them on the chair. She peeled off her gamey trousers and hung them on the hook. Under the bed was a porcelain chamber pot. She didn't know where the outhouse was and hadn't realized her need to go until she saw the simple chipped basin.

After she had relieved herself, she heard a light rap on the door. A mousy young girl of about fifteen entered the room. Her big round eyes widened when her gaze fell on Sara.

"Hello, my name is Emma. What's your name?" She placed the tray of food on the bed, meat with bread.

"Raven. Why?"

"Just curious. Trying to be polite. We don't get too many girls here. Are you alone?"

Sara only considered her feast. She wasn't interested in a conversation. Yet, the chatty girl didn't seem willing to leave.

"I saw you come in. Never seen anyone like you around here. You dress like a man." She lowered her head as if she'd spoken out of turn.

"What do you mean?" Sara asked. She tore off a piece of bread and chewed without tasting it. The dough was still warm and melted on her tongue.

"Girls like us don't travel these parts alone. There are Indians and rustlers and the like. We don't go anywhere unescorted."

Emma reached up for Sara's holsters.

"Don't touch them." Sara speared the meat with a fork and practically swallowed the juicy lump without chewing. Emma giggled when she saw this, which Sara found annoying. "I'm waiting for my bath and my bottle."

"Oh! Yes'm." Emma exclaimed, and then she hurried out of the room.

Sara gobbled the rest of the meal and stripped naked. When the subsequent knock finally came, she'd been stretched out on the bed for fifteen minutes and was close to dozing. She opened the door, read the shocked look on the girl's face, and laughed as Emma quickly looked away.

Emma held an uncorked bottle of whiskey topped with a shot glass. She hid her eyes with her other hand as she spoke. "The bath is down the hall and to your right. I left you a towel. I'm afraid the water isn't hot, though."

Sara snatched the bottle, gave Emma back the shot glass, and downed a mouthful of whiskey. The provocative taste coated her tongue with bitter deliciousness. She sighed gratefully as the hooch flooded her chest and belly with warmth.

Emma was running away when Sara called out. "I need something else."

"What do you need?" she asked as she timidly looked away.

Sara lifted and then dug into her trousers and produced her last coin. "Take care of my horse. He's the big black one, as black as midnight."

"Yes'm, and I will come back to empty your chamber pot." Then she darted away.

Sara took her bottle and sashayed down the hall to the porcelain tub. The water was lukewarm, but it didn't matter. She soaped up with the lye bar and dunked her head under the soothing liquid.

She had been lingering in the bathroom, drinking and singing old songs from her childhood, when a knock on the door interrupted her broken aria.

"How long you be?" A gruff, baritone voice asked.

"I'm coming out now," she announced, wrapped herself in a towel, and staggered back to her room with her bottle in hand, scarcely glancing at the slim intruder.

Once in her room, she sank into the bed. She upended the bottle, draining it of the last of its contents, and fell back on a pillow.

When the dangling bottle rolled out of her hand and clattered onto the floor, Sara didn't hear the impact because she was already dead asleep.

• • • •

IT WAS MORNING WHEN the light but insistent knocking invaded her dreamless slumber. Sara expected a hangover, but she didn't have one. Still, her mouth was drier than dust, and gooey mucus had caked her eyelashes until she rubbed them clean. She stretched with a yawn, only then realizing she hadn't a stitch on.

"Hello! Raven!" Emma was insistent. She knocked harder. "Wake up! There's a white lawman out looking for you. I heard him asking if they'd seen you at the Feed Store. His deputies are putting up Wanted posters all over the place with your face on them. At least, I think it looks like your'n."

Lawman? Shit.

Sara hadn't lived in Miller's Town long, but she understood how the white man's law worked. If a lawman found her, no jury could save her from a lynching. She would probably have to survive rape and torture first.

"How much are they asking for me?" she wondered as she sidled next to the window and peered out.

"I don't know. I can't read." Emma said. "I gotta go. Pa wants you out of here, now! He don't want no trouble with the law. I'm sorry," she said. Her footsteps quickly receded.

Outside, the main thoroughfare appeared nearly deserted. A few passersby strolled in and out of the shops, and a few horseback riders trotted easy paces down the street. She also saw a family traveling by wagon with the kids settled in the back, halting in front of the General Store.

Just then, a tall man emerged from the Feed Store. He was a broad fellow with twin guns belted on his hips. The brim of his hat shaded his features, making his face indiscernible. Sunlight glinted on the badge pinned to his vest. He carried rolled-up papers she assumed were the Wanted posters.

Sara darted across the room, snatched her worn clothes from the wall hooks, and slid into them. Her heart sped up, but she wasn't sure if it were fear or anticipation.

When she threw open the door, Emma stood on the other side with her hand poised for a light rap.

"What do you want?" Sara demanded, "Where's my horse?"

"He's outback in the stables. I want to let you know the law is coming this way."

"Thank you," Sara said. Next, she rolled her eyes back and fluttered her eyelashes as she sent images and commands to Midnight.

Emma gasped, stepping backward, more alarmed than before. "What are you doing?"

"Emma, get down here!" Her father's voice filled every crevice in the rooming house. "I knew she weren't nothin' but trouble."

"Yes, Pa." Emma did an about-face and hurried down the steps.

Sara could hear her father's heavy tread halfway up the stairs. The round proprietor pointed a meaty index finger at her and demanded, "You! Girl! Get out of my damn house!"

Sara donned her hat and bypassed the fuming gent as she descended the steps while fastening on her gun belts. She turned, taking the opposite direction of the front entrance, burst through a backdoor, and fled down the alley.

She found Midnight inside the stable. His head lifted, and his ears swiveled at her fast approach. He flooded her sight with an image that superimposed on the vision of her surroundings.

Sara understood his warning.

She slowed, realized her vulnerability in the narrow structure, and saw clandestine movement. She heard the cock of a gun hammer. Then reflexively, she dropped, rolled, aimed, and fired.

The man was young, perhaps in his early twenties, and bearded. He wore a star on his chest. His eyes widened, and his mouth gaped open.

Suddenly, blood saturated his shirt and covered his badge. He fell with astonishment, frozen on his face.

Sara retrieved her horse, led him onto the street, and was preparing to mount when a crowd, drawn by gunfire, gathered.

She was surrounded.

The mass turned into a mob as their anger swelled into overt outrage. The yelling, screaming, and demands for justice melded into a nearly tangible wave of horror and loathing.

"Hold it! You are under arrest!" A voice boomed, quieting the clamor.

Sara dismounted and held up her hands.

The lawman trained his gun on her face and scowled while the number of onlookers increased but kept their distance.

She recognized the broad male as the poster-toting sheriff.

He spat a wad of tobacco at her feet.

"Goddam you! He was only a kid," he yelled, as rage creased his features while he centered his aim. "I'm going to put you down like the mongrel you are!"

"Calling you out! Or are you afraid of a girl!" Sara boldly challenged, sidestepping from Midnight. "Coward!"

She slipped a hand downward, inches from her gun. Her heart pounded her ribcage, but not from fear. She was elated, anxious to see whether his head would explode when she pumped it with lead.

"Try it," he challenged. "Please do."

In the sudden quiet, she heard his gun's hammer click.

Then, a single blackbird flew across the pale blue sky in seemingly slow motion. Sara blinked once and received its presence as a sign. She promised herself the raven's loud squawk would be the last sound the lawman heard.

The gun slid out of her right holster with lightning ease. She shot without fully extending her arm. The weapon recoiled, but her stance remained rigid.

The bullet pierced the tin man's skull and exited the back of his head. A single trickle of blood dribbled from the hole in his forehead.

He was dead before he hit the ground.

Emma screamed a warning and pointed upward.

Sara turned in a flash to the spot where the young girl indicated.

Seconds later, Sara shot a man as he positioned himself on the roof. He grabbed his chest, toppled over, and landed on the ground with a hard thud.

Stunned murmurs invaded the crowd as anger turned to fear, as the townsfolk began to disburse.

Sara wasted no time as she mounted her horse. Midnight galloped as swiftly as the wind.

And the legend of Raven was born.

17. GOODBYES

SAMMY

• • • •

SAMMY CHEWED ON A FINGERNAIL while waiting patiently to awaken from the absurd dream. She thought of how Nelson's rich cologne was similar to the expensive brand her father preferred. Not a good thing.

She looked up once from her gnawed tips and saw his patient gaze. His sensuality smoldered in a way that reminded her of a young Marlon Brando.

He'd grown older while she'd languished in hell. His boyish appeal had evolved into masculine maturity. But he had the same gray eyes fringed with dark lashes that she found incredibly alluring.

She was afraid to speak, afraid even to breathe—if the truth were known—fearing her wonderful dream would evaporate. So, she sat opposite Nelson at a secluded table in the Rec Room while absurdity buzzed around them like meandering drones.

Finally, he spoke, "How are you doing?"

She chuckled and ignored the stupid question. Instead, she asked, "Where have you been?"

"I know, and I'm sorry," He said, sounding sincere.

Sammy knew even if he said nothing, he had a girlfriend. Of course, he had a girlfriend. Someone he could hold and touch and fuck. Why did it matter? They'd never even had one single date before the car accident ruined her life.

"Did you go back to Debi?" Sammy asked, although she didn't think her heart could suffer his answer. He was alive. She just existed, if you could call living in Summerhill that.

"No," he said. "Debi was never my type. I do have a girlfriend, though."

Sammy could feel her face flush, a sure sign she was close to tears. But she wouldn't cry. What did she expect? Nelson wasn't made of iron.

"I'm happy you've found someone. I'm glad you've gone on with your life." It was a sweet lie. "Thanks for telling me the truth."

Her only thought was how the last good remnant of her previous existence had been flushed down the commode of her hopeless predicament. She drew her feet onto the chair, hugged her knees, and hoped they muffled the sounds of her breaking heart.

"I wish things could've been different for us. I can't stop thinking about you and all the things you've gone through."

Sammy snapped, "I don't want your damn pity!"

He recoiled at her tone. "I don't pity you. I love you. I wish I didn't. I wish I could stop." He mumbled, "It feels like poison, sometimes."

"Thanks," she said sadly. Perhaps she should've been elated to hear his declaration, but as she stared into his gray eyes, she knew he was there for another reason. She just knew.

"Is this the part where I fall on my knees and say I love you too?" She turned away quickly so he wouldn't see her eyes misting.

His cologne filled her with an overwhelming longing. Truthfully, she wanted him to go away.

The lull in their conversation was unbearable.

Finally, she asked, "What is it you're not telling me? Is it worse than you fucking someone else? Someone you don't love?"

"I'm on break from Harvard," he blurted. A proud smile appeared but quickly faded. "I should have told you about being away at school before now. That's why I was gone so long."

Harvard? I was supposed to go to Harvard, too, she thought. However, attending the prestigious university had primarily been her dad's dream. But it had been a good one that promised a lifetime of success.

She imagined how she must've looked to him as wide-eyed astonishment devolving into full-blown sorrow. She swallowed hard—the hurt ricocheted in her chest.

"Well," she snarked. "It's not like you came here on the regular, now, is it?" Then she added sullenly, "You keep drifting from me, and it's not fair."

"You will never lose me, Sammy. We will always be better friends. I will write to you often. I promise."

Friends? Jesus Christ, go away already! Leave me with some dignity.

She wished she could scream without consequence. This time she couldn't stop the tears from rolling nonstop down her face.

"I have to go," she announced and rose. For a second, she wasn't sure if her knees would support her or if her legs would move.

Nelson was by her side, and then he wrapped her in his arms. Again, she was overwhelmed by his overtly masculine scent. His embrace was strong yet comforting. She rested her cheek on his broad shoulder and sobbed her anguish.

"I'm sorry," he said. "I needed to tell you that I still love you. It's been haunting me. I promise we will be together one day. Just get better."

Sammy whispered, "Don't sell me your bullshit. I don't want your friendship or your promises. It hurts too much. Just leave me the fuck alone."

He crushed her to his chest. "Are you sure? This isn't what I want. It just feels like I'm supposed to be with you. You're meant to be in my life. Honestly, I don't know why I have this connection to you."

She suffered a flash of her conversation with Dr. Amari, where he'd mentioned some gibberish about previous lives, then she dismissed the insanity of reincarnation.

Nelson murmured his adoration in her ear and buried his face in her hair. Suddenly, he grabbed a handful of her thick mane and, with a hard yank, forced her to stare into his eyes.

She parted her lips and accepted his passionate kiss. Sammy draped her arms around him as her ardor magnified tenfold.

He tasted sweet, like bubble gum. She moaned low in her throat when he slipped his tongue into her mouth.

Hal, the wiry orderly who filled his uniform like a coat hanger, crossed the room. He was likable because he could easily break out into a goofy smile.

"Time's up," he said as he separated them and led Sammy away.

Her heart continued shattering as she gave Nelson a desperate backward glance.

"I will write to you," he promised.

"Okay," she said, knowing it was probably a lie.

18. OPEN SPACES

*****SARA*****

• • • •

SARA'S THOUGHT WAS always the same. *I hate this world. I don't belong in it.*

And while she and Midnight roamed the West, she also realized she didn't have a true destination. As the nights grew longer and colder, she knew they needed to find refuge before winter settled. So where could she seek shelter when her bloody past forced her to avoid towns, forts, and people?

As she aimlessly wandered, she guided Midnight on underused paths. Main thoroughfares promised people, but undesirables primarily used the overgrown trails. She was also aware of an unmistakable hostility commonly shared by the ragtag travelers. While a lone rider wasn't feared or suspected, a pack of two or more tended to behave with the ferocity of wolves.

Sara hid her gender by tucking her hair under her hat and flattened her ample bosom with a swathe of torn fabric from a soon-after discarded shirt. And a downward tilt of her head at the right time also hid her feminine features.

Unfortunately, she had learned to alter her manner and appearance after a memorable encounter with four banditos on horseback. The pack had signaled their malicious intent by leering as she and Midnight headed in the opposite direction. As she neared them on the trail, she looked down and away.

Her first mistake.

Then she accidentally made eye contact with one of the riders.

Her second mistake.

And she continued riding without looking back.

Her final mistake.

A bullet tore open a hole inches from her spine. The jolt had knocked her off Midnight and dislodged her hat. Despite the excruciating pain, she rolled in the tall grass where she couldn't easily be tracked and drew her gun.

"Done tol' you that weren't no boy!" A gruff voice spat, "Even if'n it was, I ain't had a poke in a while. Why did you kill it? We coulda had some fun."

When the desperados rode closer to her hiding place and dismounted, Midnight rose on his hind legs and kicked a front leg, striking one in the head and trampling him until he stopped moving.

Meanwhile, Sara drew her six-shooter and pumped bullets into the other three with blinding speed, Bang, Bang, BANG.

Two died instantly. The last man scrambled into his saddle and sped off with his horse kicking up dirt clods.

Sara was too wounded to give chase and cursed herself for the poor aim. Rising took effort. She nearly collapsed from the pain when she twisted to examine her wound. Predictably, the beads around her neck grew warm. She felt the heat drip through her skin, melt into her blood and solidify inside the hole producing her agony. Slowly, the severe injury devolved into a dull ache and then a pinprick of annoyance.

She picked through the dead men's saddlebags and confiscated their dried food, and filled up her canteen with their water. She was especially pleased when she found bottles of whiskey. She popped the cork on one bottle and took a swig. The liquor was bitter and potent, but not the good stuff as if that mattered.

Then she unsaddled their horses and freed them with slaps to their backsides before mounting her beloved steed.

She and Midnight continued south. Eventually, the flat topography changed from grassy fields and thick forests. Too many times, she also happened upon the sad remnants of battles. The dead, rotting bodies were often Natives among a smattering of whites. No matter. She scavenged the dead for anything she could use: coins, tobacco, matches.

Once, she discovered a burnt-out wagon train shot full of arrows. She spent hours foraging through the settlers' belongings. She explored each burnt wagon, sometimes overstepping the hacked or scalped remains for supplies.

The horses were always gone, possibly taken by the Natives. Still, she found a travel-worthy wagon and hitched it to her horse. After most attacks, the food was seized, but she had earned some good luck in one instance. She discovered provisions, mostly beans, flour, wheat, and jerky. Next, she filled her wagon with bolts of cloth and broken wood bits from the other wagons so she could effortlessly start campfires.

By now, the days were shorter and colder. Encouraged by the amount and quality of her loot, she decided to find a place for the winter. She didn't know where, but she knew someone, or *something*, who could help.

That night, after a good meal, she drank half a bottle of a dead man's whiskey. Then she slept in the wagon atop yards of bleached sheeting.

Where can I go?

She wasn't sure if she was asleep or awake or someplace between. In her dream-wake state, her slight movements were akin to maneuvering underwater. Even her long tresses floated around her face as if she were swimming in fluids.

She descended the wagon's steps, but she wasn't sure if she walked or floated.

Stuuwi, I know you're here. I know it was you who helped me before, and I need your help now.

The burning woman materialized next to a tree as if she'd always been close.

I'm not a trickster. You are. You know much and forget most.

Sara took an involuntary backward step. The creature was frighteningly near, and the way she stared with fire leaping from her eye sockets caused Sara's fear to ratchet up several notches.

A patch of seared meat slid off the Stuuwi's shoulder, revealing a slick square of muscle and tendon. Despite the sooty mess covering her face, Sara realized something about the creature's face that reminded her of her mother, Ruthie.

As if reading her thoughts, the Stuuwi laughed. As she did so, her mouth stretched abnormally from ear to ear like a macabre totem of an evil deity.

Sara, who embraced her life with a measure of fearlessness, was terrified to the core of the nether creature.

She challenged. "You're not my mother. Stop wearing my mother's face!"

Am I wearing your mother's face? Are you sure?

Instantly quiet, Sara tried to snuff her confusion.

Do you want my help? You have your immortality. What more do you want? The voice hissed in her head while her sardonic grin lengthened into a toothless and cavernous hole. Suddenly, a burst of hollow laughter echoed from her mouth.

Sara recoiled and took another involuntary backward step. Or was she swimming? "I didn't ask for immortality. Survival is not the same as living," She retorted, trying to sound brave.

The Stuuwi's meat sizzled as the fire ringed her bald head and licked her scalp displaying patches of her white skull. The raw combination of burning flesh and boiling blood filled Sara's nostrils. She turned her head to avoid the assaulting odor when she noticed her body fitfully sleeping in the wagon.

She gasped at the incredible absurdity of her nightmare.

What is done is done. What do you want from me?

The entity's communication interrupted Sara's captivation by the eerie view, and her first thought centered on Little Ruthie. Still, she couldn't sully her child's existence by asking for something as selfish as a reunion. Instead, she asked, *I want a home.*

The creature moved forward, and again, Sara took a backward step.

I can't give you a home, but I can show you where to stay for the winter.

Sara said, "I guess that will have to be enough. For now."

The fiery woman soared gracefully in the air and landed inches from Sara. Before she could react, the creature slapped a burning palm on Sara's forehead.

The touch seared through Sara's skin. The agony drove into her skull and inflamed her brain. She tried to free herself, but she couldn't move. She screamed even as an image formed in her mind—she pictured a sod house needing repair. And the location? Yes, she knew where to find it. The house sat in an isolated canyon near a clear stream which was perfect for a wayward outlaw.

Do you see it?

"Yes," she answered, gasping for breath as the stench of burning rot clogged her nostrils.

Then go, Trickster. As the evil thing faded, she taunted Sara with an echoing jeer. *I know what you don't know. Yet.*

• • • •

SHE AWOKE SWATHED IN unnerving terror. Yet the sod house's route remained imprinted in her mind.

In only a day's ride, she and Midnight reached their destination. The dwelling looked better than it had in her nightmare.

The construction was a simple abode dug into the earth. The mud shack wasn't too different from the lodge houses of her childhood. Only this time, someone had plastered over the sod walls, possibly trying to keep out vermin.

Sara loved the isolation amid rolling hills and snow-capped mountains. As expected, when she opened the door, there was evidence of a brutal slaughter. Blood splatters had dried on some of the meager furnishings, and gory pools stretched across the dirt floor like carpeting.

She wasn't skittish. She was accustomed to the aftermath of massacres. She looked beyond the violence and concentrated on the soundness of the house. Although it was nothing special: sod bricks, a window, and a wooden roof, she now considered it home.

The bed and table had been built into the walls. In a dugout, a sort of closet, she found a sewing machine and a butter churn. Behind the sod house was a smaller dwelling, which she planned to use for Midnight's lodging.

She searched the left-behind scraps and found a block of soap and a broom. She spent the day washing down walls and cleaning furnishings. She emptied her wagon, used bits of it for firewood, and prepared an outdoor feast. Midnight chose to sleep outside instead of the small box next to the house. No matter, she would fix it up for him. In the meantime, she celebrated in her new home with a half-full bottle of whiskey.

19. REFUGE IN NYSA

• • • •

SAMMY STOOD ON THE jagged cliff with her toes digging into the dewy grass. The brilliant sunlight and spray from the waterfall formed a glorious rainbow that glimmered opposite her perch. She saw rainbows arching over the waterfall as she glanced down at the foamy water exploding on the rocks below.

Nysa. Home. Refuge from Hell.

She flung her arms wide as if ready to embrace the sun that beamed warmth on her skin like golden kisses. Then, floating on the gentle breeze, she caught the acrid odor of manure. The smell was an alien and certainly unwanted intrusion in her utopia. She turned toward the scent and was shocked.

Sara gave her a quizzical look. Her smile was slow to surface. "I didn't expect to see you here."

"Okay, you stink. Ew, you smell just like shit!"

"Nice," Sara said. "And you smell like sickness."

"I deserved that," she replied.

In truth, she was alarmed by Sara's appearance. Her twin, although muscular, looked malnourished. Even her eyes appeared too large in her gaunt face. Despite their safety in Nysa, Sammy noticed something predatory in Sara's stance. It was as if she were on constant alert, ready to pounce and then shred.

Sara lifted a corner of her pouty lips until she wore a menacing sneer. "I smell your fear. Why are you afraid of me?"

"Smell my fear? Really? Kind of out there, don't you think?" Nevertheless, Sammy inched safely from the ledge.

"I don't know what you mean," Sara said. And then, without warning, she jumped into a high-flying kick. Her dark hair trailed her impromptu assault like delicate black gossamer. The soft appearance of her hair was incongruent with the harshness etched on her features.

Sammy wasn't caught unaware. The glint in Sara's eye had telegraphed her intention. Sammy dodged the blow.

There was a millisecond when she considered fighting back, but she hightailed it instead. Her world was collapsing, and she needed Nysa for rejuvenation.

Sara grabbed her tresses and spun Sammy around. Then she threw a right hook, which Sammy blocked with the heel of her hand. Then, in a flash, she punched Sara in the face.

"You're too slow, kiddo." Sammy teased. "Put some damn meat on your bones."

Sara swiped the bloody trails dribbling from her nostrils and pounced by kneeing Sammy in the gut.

Sammy doubled over and then dropped to her knees. Sara closed in, and when she was near enough, Sammy punched up and then out. Sara fell backward. Sammy tried to catch her breath as she sprang to her feet and aimed her raised foot at Sara's head.

Before Sammy could deliver the blow, Sara rolled out of the way and climbed to her feet. She tried to land an uppercut.

Sammy ducked and swerved, firing a flurry of punches until a left hook sent Sara spinning. The fight moved into the woods and only ended when Sammy was beaten down to her knees. Sara grabbed Sammy's shoulders, ready to knee her face when Sammy clobbered her twin's vagina with a raised knuckle.

"Ow!" Sara clutched the spot.

Sammy, huffing from exertion, screamed, "Enough! Okay? Damn!" Then, she stood and slapped Sara's face. "That's for being a bitch! So yeah, it's called a bitch slap!"

Sara, still holding her crotch, assented with a nod.

After she calmed down, Sammy asked. "What's going on with you? You look like shit, and you smell like shit too. Don't you bathe?"

Sara's lower lip quivered as tears rolled down her cheeks. "It's hard. Midnight and I are surviving, but life is hard. I wish to die sometimes. Clyde is gone. The townies murdered him."

"Oh no!" Sammy drew Sara into an embrace.

Sara shrugged herself free. Sometimes kindness was too painful. "I can be myself with you. I don't have to pretend to be...."

"...Tough?" Sammy finished. "I hope you are always your true self with me." Then she added, "What happened to Clyde? Why did they kill him?"

Sara said, shuddering, "I can't talk about it yet. He was a good man, though. I should've gotten him out."

Sammy understood the implication that Sara had done something, and Clyde had paid with his life. She changed the subject, although not in the best way. "Do you think about Little Ruthie?"

Sara admitted, "I try not to. I didn't think I could miss her. Until I gave birth, she was just a thing in my body. My mother lost twelve of her babies. I can survive losing one."

"Twelve," she muttered. "Jesus, I can't imagine."

Sara asked, "Do you think of your lost little one?"

This time, it was Sammy who wept. "I don't remember his face. I know I gave him a name, but I can't remember it now. I mean, they fried my brain and took those memories from me."

Sara took Sammy's hand in hers. "Fried your brain? I don't understand."

Sammy didn't know how to explain without a convoluted discussion on electricity. Instead, she said, "It's a way of wiping someone's memory so they can forget the hard stuff."

"You can do this?" Sara squeezed her hand. "There is hard stuff I wish to forget. But why do you ask about the little ones?"

Sammy shrugged. "I keep having this dream about my mom visiting me and holding my baby. Although I can't see any definition on his face, I still think it's a sweet dream. Then I wake up, and my whole life feels worse."

"We have each other," Sara said.

"Yes," Sammy agreed.

They hugged and sealed their solidarity. Their closeness felt right. Sammy didn't even mind Sara's shitty smell.

"Y'know," she said, as she stared into Sara's eyes, "Dr. Asshole thinks you're a figment of my imagination. If I want to get out, I have to convince him I don't believe in you."

Sara repeated, "I don't understand."

"Yeah, you do," Sammy said. As she looked deeply into Sara's eyes, she found their uncanny resemblance a bit chilling. Not only did they look alike, but Sara occasionally mimicked Sammy's expressions.

Sara wiped Sammy's face and gave her a lazy grin. This time her smile was warm and endearing. "I feel better now. It's good to hear another voice. Midnight is a lot of things, but he's a terrible conversationalist."

They punctuated their laughter with identical snorts. First, Sara reclined on the grass, then Sammy. They stared at the puffy white globs floating in a sea of blue.

"Where are you?" Sammy asked.

"In the territory. I've found a little house, and there are books. Someone who used to live in the house was a reader. I've read Moby Dick and The Scarlett Letter. There are more books to keep me company."

"They moved out and left their books?"

"They were killed. I suppose wolves scavenged their bodies. I haven't found any remains." Sara shrugged. "I did find some arrows, but I can't tell if they belonged to the Cheyenne or Sioux?"

Sammy thought, *Oh my God!*

Sara said, "I want to live and not survive. Where can I go? Where can I be happy?"

"Didn't you tell me once that your mother said you would find happiness with some man with blue eyes?" Sammy asked. She plucked a blade of grass and gnawed. "Maybe you should look for him."

Sara's voice was as hard as stone. "I don't trust blue eyes."

Sammy turned to look at her and again saw rigidity settle on Sara's features. "You trust Violet."

Sara spat, "She didn't save Clyde."

"I bet she tried."

Sammy knew she had to help Sara find a safe place. "Do you know what year you're in? I can look up something on the computer and tell you the best place for you to live. But America is not exactly safe for me either."

"Year?" Sara mouthed the words, *computer,* and *America*. "Your words are strange."

"Never mind," Sammy said, "I will try to approximate from some of the things you've already told me."

Sammy spat the blade of grass. Her thoughts drifted to Nelson. "Maybe you're right. Anyone waiting for a man to make them happy is fucked. We have to make ourselves happy."

"Agreed," Sara said. Then she added, "I've made something for you."

She lifted her leg, reached inside her dirty boot, and pulled out a beaded necklace. The stones glimmered like precious gems. Each bead seemed to have a little light swirling inside. When the Stuuwi burned me, she told me where to live and left me with the ability to make it. I think she did it on purpose."

"The Stuuwi burned you?" Sammy said, then she recoiled. "Is that what I think it is? You made this?"

"Yes, this one time and right after I woke up. I can't remember how I did it now." Sara said.

Before Sammy could protest, Sara leaned over her and placed the necklace on her throat, where it unrolled unassisted.

"Jesus!" Sammy swore as the damnable thing slithered and fastened. "What have you done!"

Sammy sat, yanked, and pulled as she swore. The necklace elongated or snapped back in place at her desperate tugs and jerks, but she could not remove it.

"Why!" Sammy screamed. "Fucking thing feels like a goddam noose! Take it off!"

Sara shook her head."Maybe this thing will be gone when I'm back in the nuthouse." At least she was comforted by that hope.

Sara said, "Mother always said I was powerful because my father was a medicine man, and she was a priestess. Nysa is magical. I think we can take some of the magic outside this world."

"I don't believe you." Sammy continued to weep.

"Then why are you crying?" She squinted. "You're not telling me something." Sara scanned Sammy's face. "You've seen her, haven't you? The Stuuwi."

"No," Sammy lied. Then she asked, "Suppose you're right. Why did you do this to me? You hate being immortal, so why do you want me to be the same way."

Sara regarded Sammy as if she were a fool. "I don't want you to die. I never want to lose you like I lost Clyde."

COLD-BLOODED RINGERS

20. BASS REEVES

••••

BASS REEVES STRODE into the courtroom with heavy, unhurried steps, and as soon as he entered, the subdued chatter in the room hushed. Judge Isaac Parker looked up from the papers on his bench and gave the imposing black male a half-smile as a silent greeting. Bass returned a slight nod of acknowledgment.

The delicate clicking of his spurs was the only audible sound in court until he took a seat in the back of the room. The day was hot. The courthouse atmosphere didn't offer any respite from the heat.

He removed his hat and mopped his forehead with a handkerchief. As he tucked the damp cloth in a vest pocket, the defendant turned in his seat and scowled at him.

Bass only smiled and politely nodded.

Of course, the lawman recognized the worthless piece of meat as a lowlife murdering cuss. Hanging was too good for him. He had gutted a homesteader, raped the dead man's wife, and burned their cabin after stealing their meager possessions. Bass would've tracked the godless bastard to Hell. That excrement had earned his due justice at the end of a knotted rope.

The hanging judge pounded his gavel and sentenced the miscreant to death. The newly condemned man fought against the deputies who dragged him from the courtroom. His chains rattled as he struggled against his restraints.

"I'll get you, Bass!" he screamed.

Sure. How often had he heard the same declaration from scum who mocked the law?

The next defendant was a thin-faced, raggedy-toothed horse thief. Yes, Bass recognized him, too. Catching the wily bandit had been a bit of a chore. Although he looked ignorant, the crook had proven to be quite elusive. It was a good thing his Native friend was an excellent tracker.

Bass saw how the court of the damned was in full swing. He considered leaving and moseying down to the General Store where it was apt to be cooler but nixed the idea. After all, the judge had summoned him, and he owed the man his allegiance and his job. A cold drink on a hot day could wait.

Hours later, and during a lull in the proceedings, Judge Parker motioned for him to come forward.

"Good afternoon, Judge. How's Mary?" Bass asked once he stood at the bench.

"The wife is fine. I would ask you to stop over, but I need you to find someone right away."

He motioned to a deputy who rifled through a set of papers on a desk nearest the judge's seat. The young man retrieved one from the pile, a Wanted poster, and handed it to the lawman.

Bass scanned the poster and looked up with a quizzical expression on his handsome face.

"Raven? A Native girl?" Bass asked. "Murder?"

"Murders." The judge corrected. "She has a taste for lawmen, so *you* be careful. Burned down half a town, Miller's Town, heard of it?"

"Yeah, enough to avoid it."

"Bring her back alive if you can. I want to make an example of her."

• • • •

THERE WAS PEACE IN isolation. In Sara's contentment, she'd grown careless. The day in the gulch was like any other. A severe winter had melted into an early Spring. First, she fed and watered Midnight, and then, taking her makeshift rod to the creek, she hoped to catch a fish for breakfast.

She sandwiched the stick between two large rocks and leaned over the clear waters where she thought she saw blue catfish. Her mouth watered. She caught her reflection and remembered Sammy's teases. Now she was in the habit of bathing.

Sammy. She tried not to think about how unwell Sammy had looked. Or the things they were doing to her in the place she called a hospital.

Sara also remembered how Sammy's eyes had often lost focus. During their brief time in Nysa, Sammy had drooled, and her broken sentences had drifted into heartbreaking silence. She had mumbled something about "...upped the dosages of my meds." Sara had no idea what that meant, but she was glad she'd ambushed Sammy with the necklace and possibly saved her life.

Sara yawned, scratched, and stretched lazily in the bright morning light. Her bare toes dug into the yielding mud at the water's edge. Oozing earth squirted between the digits. She hitched up her skirt of sweeping gingham, one of many items she'd found in the house, and scooped out a handful of cold water. She splashed water on her face and wiped with the hem of her skirt.

Suddenly, Midnight neighed. His excitement tasted like fear.

Sara froze, her happiness melting like snow in Summer. Suddenly, she noticed the absurd quiet. Not even a bird chirped. She pretended a calm she didn't feel while recognizing her vulnerability. She was weaponless. Her guns, blade, and brass knuckles were inside the house.

She cursed her stupidity. Tranquility had lulled her into foolishness. She did an easy about-face and was ready to bolt the thirty-odd steps to her home.

His badge glinted in the sun as he emerged from the nearby curtain of thick trees. He was astride a stallion with a gleaming white coat, a beast as exceptional as her well-muscled Midnight. She didn't need to read the script on his bronze star to know he was the law. Yet, she was taken aback because his skin was black.

He dismounted and walked towards her.

He was tall, more than six feet, and imposing. Although his smile wasn't menacing under his thick black mustache, his eyes narrowed as he closed the distance between them.

"Morning," he said cordially and tipped his hat. "Nice weather for fishing."

She couldn't pretend an easiness she didn't feel. Just then, a Native man straddling a dappled horse trotted from around her abode. His stern features offered no doubt of their intentions. He freed his gun deftly.

Once again, Sara silently cursed her carelessness. She knitted her brows as she looked from one to the other. She refused to surrender by raising her hands.

The marshal unfolded a worn poster and examined the image, and while his smile remained warm, his eyes lacked compassion.

"Raven," he said after a great sigh. "My name is Bass Reeves. As a duly sworn deputy of the Indian Territory, I am placing you under arrest."

The Native man dismounted, which was the moment she had awaited. The marshal folded the poster, reached into his pocket, and pulled out a set of irons.

She leaped and kicked the black man in the groin. He muffled a groan as he doubled over and grabbed his genitals.

She pivoted and, with a swift jolt of her leg, kicked the gun out of the Native's hand. She heard the marshal creep behind her, so she spun around and side-kicked his guts. When he doubled over, she kneed his face. He flailed backward and landed on his posterior.

The Native lunged for his gun. Sara jumped on his back and cradled his neck inside the crook of her arm. He struggled and bucked, but her hold on him remained steadfast. As he gurgled for breath, his splayed fingers reached forward to grab his weapon.

Sara heard the click of the marshal's gun. She lifted his partner's torso as her shield. Her smile was filled with menace as she tightened her hold on the Native. The stalemate continued as he grew limp in her arm.

"Back up," Sara said. It was a simple command. "Or I will kill him."

"So, you *do* speak English?" The lawman holstered his gun and raised both his hands. "You can't escape the law."

"What law?" Sara asked. "I don't recognize your laws."

The Native man grew quiet and slumped in her tightening embrace.

The conversation was a ruse. When her attention focused on the marshal, her captive had grabbed a handful of dirt. He flung it into her eyes. While she was temporarily blinded, he wedged his hand between her arm and his throat and flipped her to the ground.

Her vision cleared a millisecond before seeing the marshal's fist. She saw sparks and felt raw pain before everything went dark.

• • • •

SHE WAS ASTRIDE MIDNIGHT, chained at the wrists like an animal, broiling under the merciless sun. She was sandwiched between her captors while they clip-clopped on the rugged terrain.

She couldn't move freely. The manacles were heavy and scraped her skin raw. The only thing she could do was hold the reins and grip the saddle horn. At least they allowed her to change clothing. Once again, she dressed like a boy. It was always better to travel as a male.

Occasionally the two men would converse in a low fraternal chatter. She sensed more than simple companionship between them. They seemed like brothers.

Mostly, they traveled speedily through the terrain by taking direct routes to places Sara had always avoided. Usually, the group would arrive at some fort before nightfall. Once there, she was locked up in a cage. Her care was then left to the soldier on guard duty. Not all of the soldiers were kind, but she understood they were respectful to her because of him.

Bass Reeves.

She heard his name intoned with a thread of fear. At least being captured by the big man earned her a modicum of safety. Mostly she was the lone occupant in a usually dank cell. Other times, the prisoner in the next cell would give her reverence. She wondered if it was because she had merited capture by a legend.

Sara tried to calculate her escape.

She never spoke.

She only watched and waited.

She ate the slop served on tin plates. She drank the gritty water and relieved herself in a bucket, sometimes while the men watched. She sat cross-legged on the mattress until she grew tired enough to sleep. Yet, no one could get close without her eyelids opening. Her bleary gaze would instantly harden like steel. In the mornings, her escorts would appear, and their exhausting journey would begin anew.

The weariness weighed down her bones. In her weakened state, the iron manacles easily tipped her over. The procession would stop, and they would find shade and take a break. Then, after their respite, she mounted her horse and followed Bass to their next destination.

Midnight was always rested and well-fed, and her gratitude to her captors grew. Sometimes, during breaks, and despite the awkwardness, she ran her dirty fingers along his face. He would place his nose on her neck as gently as a sweet kiss.

Bass allowed their silent communication. Too many times, she ached to ride him to freedom. Only then did tears form, leaving clean streaks on her grimy face. Always, she murmured words of endearment whenever she had the chance to press her face against his soft black coat.

Family. He was all she had left, at least in this world. So she was unashamed of the rare spectacle.

There were times, not many, when they had to camp under the stars. The men unsaddled the horses and took turns starting a fire and cooking a pot of meat and beans. The native, whom Bass called Grant, would disappear and reappear just as Bass piled food on tin plates. Whenever he returned, he would give Bass a slight nod. Sara understood his signal meant they were safe from any riffraff who populated the territory.

The men shoveled food into their mouths and talked amongst themselves as if she were of no consequence. She usually sat cross-legged near the fire. She unusually consumed a few bites of food, sipped the bitter coffee, and then while staring at the flames, she rolled her eyes back in her head. She spent the rest of the evening conversing with Midnight.

Her horse, tethered nearby with the others, would respond with either a neigh or a shake of his massive head. And when he profoundly disagreed, he would stomp a hoof on the dirt.

Sometimes she laughed at the pictures he sent to her. Usually, they were silly things he'd witnessed in the forts. Comical things people did when they assumed no one was watching, like pissing in a drink and handing it to someone else to gulp.

After her evening chats with Midnight, she would roll her eyes straight. Always, she found the lawmen staring with blank expressions on their faces. After the meal, they unfurled their bedrolls. Sara was forced into shackles before she was draped with a blanket.

Late one cold night, as Bass doused the campfire to lessen their chances of being ambushed, he eyed her with suspicion.

Sara stretched out under a blanket. The ground was hard and rocky. She couldn't find any comfort, especially with the manacles and shackles chafing her skin raw.

"You talk to your horse?" Bass asked.

The unexpected question startled her. "Yes. He's my family."

"He's a fine horse. I will make sure to find him a good home."

The chirping crickets filled the silence, and somewhere an owl hooted.

Sara smirked and then rolled onto her side. The meaning of his words quickened her heart, but only for a moment. Her composure came from the hopeful truism of her immortality.

She said, "There's no need for you to find my horse a good home, Mr. Reeves. You've been kind to me and Midnight. I won't seek you out and kill you."

Bass exploded with rich laughter. Grant, who had listened to the exchange, studied Sara and didn't make a sound.

Sara drifted to sleep with Bass's chuckles resounding in her ears.

COLD-BLOODED RINGERS

21. A HANGING

SARA

....

THE TRIO RODE THROUGH the Western District of Arkansas until they ended their dusty trek in Fort Smith. As they trotted the main street, white ladies smiled, and men tipped their hats to the tall black man astride his white steed.

Sara was led to a courthouse and taken downstairs to a basement jail. A powerful stench immediately overcame her. She saw only two cells crammed with only men who openly leered at her with either disgust or lust. The combined stink from the filthy ruffians settled on her like a cloud. And she coughed, hoping to dislodge the knot of foul that had lumped in her throat.

"Welcome to Hell on the Border," Bass said as he unfastened her manacles. "I wish I had someplace else to hold you, but I don't."

He opened the door and announced to the men, in a booming baritone, "If anyone touches her, I will shoot you myself and save the judge the trouble of a hanging. I mean what I say. Understood?"

There were some murmurs but more discords and guffaws crammed with cussing and swearing.

He slipped out his gun and held it up. The weapon gleamed in the diminished light. "I said, *understood*?"

This time the mumbling agreements were louder.

Sara was grateful, but she knew better. She was tough, but there was no way she could protect herself. And she guessed there were roughly fifty men in each cell.

Still, she entered with her head held up while keeping her face emotionless. The prison door clanged with harsh finality. A guard turned the locking mechanism, and Bass disappeared up the stairs.

They ogled her as she made her way to the rear and pressed her back against the stone wall. The prisoners didn't make a sound. Instead, they moved like a wave, each one following her movements.

Meanwhile, the young, slim guard pulled up a chair and sat outside spitting distance from the cells.

"Y'all heard what Bass said." His squeaky voice tried to sound authoritative, "I don't want no shit happening on my watch cuz of some red nigger squaw!"

Her safety was an illusion. Sara knew this. She refused the food, globs of white paste, and corn and wet herself instead of using the urinal.

That night, Sara refused to sleep. Instead, she sat on the floor, again with her back against the wall, and drew her knees to her chest.

Soon after sunlight crept into the pits the following morning, a guard called her name. After being cuffed and shackled, she was marched upstairs into the courtroom. After spending all day and evening in the dark cell, she rapidly blinked to adjust to the sun-filled room.

A stern-faced man in a black robe sat stiffly in a leather chair. His thick brown hair and goatee were neatly trimmed, and he pierced her with a harsh appraisal.

"You look younger than your picture," he said, chewing on his dismay.

Sara remained mute.

The jury filed into the courtroom, all white and all men. Too many blatantly wore their disgust.

The prosecutor, a jowly codger, called their witnesses. The first on the stand was the deputy she'd failed to kill in Harmony. Next were residents from Miller's Town. One old coot scowled as he explained how she'd "damn near" burned down the whole town.

Did she have a defense?

A skinny and anxious man Sara had never seen before admitted he needed time to confer with his client.

She chimed at the indignity of it all. "I don't recognize the white man's laws."

Her words carried in the silent courtroom, and soon after, menacing grumblings erupted.

Without fanfare, her trial was over. An overfed jurist announced her guilt. The judge pounded his gavel when a cheerful uproar met his declaration and quieted the onlookers.

Judge Parker sighed, "Raven, you are sentenced to hang until you are dead."

Sara's eyes drifted to the gallows positioned just outside the courtroom. A repressed memory surfaced. She'd seen a man led to a tree in Miller's Town. She remembered the festivities held after his body swung from a crooked limb.

Her shudder was involuntary because she knew she would probably provide obscene entertainment to another crowd.

As she was led out, prison guards brought another unfortunate soul into the courtroom.

She was shoved back inside the cell, and after locking the door, the guard chuckled.

With her back, once again, pressed to the wall, she waited, and it was torture.

Damn! She wanted them to get on with it.

Her thin fingers caressed the necklace. She'd been healed many times, but death? But had she honestly drowned that day? Died? Maybe she was delusional to believe in a protective spirit and a strange piece of jewelry? The beads warmed her fingertips. The lights within the color orbs glowed.

Have faith, she told herself. *Don't be afraid.*

It was late afternoon when several guards trudged down the steps. The officer on duty jumped to his feet and unlocked her cell.

With his gun aimed into the crowded pen, one of the guards laughingly said, “Ladies first.”

Sara wordlessly complied.

Four other prisoners were yanked out of the cage for the five nooses. The guard pushed her as she marched up the stairs.

She ignored her rough treatment.

Instead, Sara sent Midnight a quick “where are you?” message.

He sent her images. And she saw that he stood in a comfortable looking stable.

She emerged outside, tired, lightheaded, and, yes, afraid. She raised her cuffed hand and shielded her face from the sun. But the chains rubbed the skin off her meat, making her movements difficult. And because she wasn’t moving fast enough, she was pushed along the scaffolding.

Meanwhile, the burgeoning crowd of onlookers jeered and verbally encouraged her harsh handling. Most of their constant scorn appeared aimed at her, but she remained stoic. She wouldn’t give them the satisfaction of quivering.

And as she expected, the atmosphere was eerily festive. Toddlers sat on the shoulders of fathers. Families arrived with the mothers toting picnic baskets. Peddlers sold candies and treats while children ran through the masses until all the condemned faced the crossbeams. Then there was utter silence.

Ladies first.

Sara was led to the first serpentine coiled noose.

A portly hangman slipped the rope roughly over her head and snaked it around her neck. Then he jerked the cord until it was a snug fit.

Suddenly, a dark cloud glided over the sunlight creating a shadow over the gallows. A blackbird loudly flapped its wings as it soared in a graceful ascent and landed just on the timber over Sara’s noose.

A raven.

She smiled.

The hangman shooed the bird, but instead of immediately flying away, it circled above the spectacle, causing some women in the crowd to shriek before soaring from view.

At last, the condemned were lined up, the rustler who had shot up a saloon, the bank robber who had killed a teller, the hired gun with rotten teeth, and the baby-faced kid who had killed his former girlfriend and her family.

Sara heard someone sniveling and peered down the row. The bank robber wept moments before the hangman plopped a hood on his head.

When it was her turn to wear the smelly head covering, she resisted with a twist of her head.

The hangman bellowed, "It ain't for you! It's so they don't have to look at your ugly face when you choke."

Sara calmly said, "I don't think they would mind."

Nevertheless, he blotted out her view with the covering. She imagined the stink was from the sweat and tears of dead men.

Fear inched along her spine when she heard the hangman's heavy footsteps move away from her and toward the lever.

There was the harsh sound of gears.

Amid a growing uproar, Sara felt the floor disappear. Instantly the rope gouged into her throat. Sara's neck snapped. And then... nothing.

End of Book 2

ABOUT THE AUTHOR

• • • •

JULIAN M. COLEMAN IS a wife, mother, and grandmother who enjoys reading, writing, and running, but not necessarily in that order. As a sufferer of night terrors, her nightmares are the source of her creativity. In other words, she never suffers from writer's block.

Don't miss out!

Visit the website below and you can sign up to receive emails whenever Julian M. Coleman publishes a new book. There's no charge and no obligation.

https://books2read.com/r/B-A-CAPD-TNMLB

BOOKS 2 READ

Connecting independent readers to independent writers.

Did you love *Cold-Blooded Ringers*? Then you should read *The Fury of Angels*[1] by Julian M. Coleman!

[2]

The twins are fierce, beautiful, and identical. Although they were born in different centuries, they found a supernatural way to coexist. They weren't born fighters, but the brutality of their parallel realities made them warriors. Will their brand new immortality withstand their ruthlessness?

An intense and historical fantasy from the JAN 2016 Outstanding Paranormal/Supernatural Book of the Year author. From the beginning of the Damned Reflections trilogy, Julian M. Coleman weaves a harsh, paranormal saga filled with betrayals, sacrifices, and bloodshed.Samantha Montgomery transfers from Jefferson High School to Ridgeway Prep. Lonesome and ostracized in the new preppy and materialistic en-

1. https://books2read.com/u/3JXg1v

2. https://books2read.com/u/3JXg1v

vironment, Sammy escapes to the Nirvana-like dreamworld she calls Nysa. She's not alone in her private heaven. Sammy shares the tropical paradise with twin Sara, a half-native teen with a murderous chip on her shoulder the size of Oklahoma.

In Sara's reality, she lives in the late 1800s. Her mother, a priestess, is a runaway slave. Her father is a respected medicine man. Sara has no friends in the village. She's harassed and ridiculed. It's a life-altering sequence -- spurned love, an attempted rape, and a spiritual (demonic) awakening after near-death – that changes the shy teen into an efficient killer.

Only Sammy's devotion quells Sara's bloodlust -- until Sammy becomes a killer too.

Read more at juliancoleman.net.

Also by Julian M. Coleman

Book 1

Stolen Prophet: The Prophet's Mother

Damned Reflections

The Fury of Angels

Cold-Blooded Ringers

The Demon Lover's Chronicles

Cesar

Cesar's Revenge

Rise of the Priestess

The Prophet's Mother

Malevolent Sadness: A Paranormal Suspense Thriller

Between False Shadows: A Paranormal Supernatural Thriller

Standalone

Really, Cher? A Story With a Dog in It
The Demon Lover's Chronicles (The Complete Series)

Watch for more at juliancoleman.net.

www.ingramcontent.com/pod-product-compliance
Lightning Source LLC
LaVergne TN
LVHW010618100826
845148LV00014B/3022

* 9 7 8 1 7 3 6 5 1 5 1 1 2 *